THE FAKE FIANCÉ'S BILLIONAIRE ADVERSARY

A CAPROCK CANYON ROMANCE BOOK TWO

BREE LIVINGSTON

Edited by

CHRISTINA SCHRUNK

The Fake Fiancé's Billionaire Adversary

Edited by Christina Schrunk

https://www.facebook.com/christinaschrunk.editor

Proofread by Krista R. Burdine

https://www.facebook.com/iamgrammaresque

Cover design by Victorine Lieske

http://victorinelieske.com/

Bree Livingston

https://www.breelivingston.com

The Fake Fiancé's Billionaire Adversary/ Bree Livingston. -- 1st ed.

ISBN: 9781700087591

This book is dedicated to Danielle Thorne. The Sandy Pelican was a great name and Reagan loved it. Thanks for the suggestion, Danielle!

CHAPTER 1

Stretching his sore arms above his head, Hunter West ignored the snaps and pops his joints were making. He wasn't even sure why he was still pushing himself like this. A little over a year ago, he'd become a billionaire. That one little lottery ticket had changed his bank account, but not his mindset. As his dad would say, the fruit of a man's labor is what keeps him young.

Besides, hard work had never bothered him. If anything, he loved flipping houses because it made him feel good to see the finished product and know it was his hands that did it. More importantly, it hid his winnings from the lottery. After seeing what happened with his older brother, Bear, he worked to keep his fortune hidden. Hunter didn't want the heartache of loving someone only to find out they wanted his money and not him.

As of late, he'd begun to wonder if his mindset didn't need a little adjusting. The joints in his thirty-four-year-old six-foot frame seemed to be hinting it might be time to call it quits. In Hunter's case, it wasn't the age but the mileage that had him thinking about hanging up his hammer and settling down, hopefully in the bed and breakfast he wanted to buy a few miles away.

"Paint's done," his partner, Stone, said as he stopped in the doorway of the bathroom Hunter was working on.

Hunter twisted at the waist to ease some of the soreness in his lower back. His shower would be hotter than usual tonight. "Yeah, Ryan told me. You knocking off for the day?" Ryan was their contractor. He'd joined the company three years ago at about the age when Hunter had started flipping houses.

"No. I want to check on that other property we're doing demo on this week." His partner's response wasn't surprising. They were always working on more than one project at a time.

In a blink, he was back to thinking about the local beachfront bed and breakfast he'd passed more than once since he'd arrived on Tybee Island, Georgia. Talk about a project. That place needed almost as much work as the houses they typically flipped.

According to rumors, The Sandy Pelican B&B wouldn't survive much longer, and it would be on the auction block. More than once, he'd caught himself fantasizing about what he'd do with the place if he bought it. Did he flip it or restore it? The latter was becoming more and more appealing. Settling down, a wife, kids, and the beach right outside his back door. Retiring from this back-breaking work.

That's, of course, if he managed to purchase the place. The retiring part of the equation was selling his half of Stone-West Housing. Hunter wasn't too bad at negotiations. Maybe he'd convince the owner of the B&B to sell it to him before it went under and then approach Stone about what to do with Hunter's half of the business. He didn't have to sell it. Winning the lottery gave him the option to keep it and hire someone, but when he retired, he wanted to be retired, not managing a flipping business.

Now, if he had the bed and breakfast, that would be different. Staying put, enjoying island life, and renting out a room now and then...there wouldn't be the stress of deadlines and permits. It would be just him and his shanty by the sea.

But selling his half of the business was a conversation for another day. "Is something wrong, or are you just checking up on it?" Hunter asked.

"Just making sure the demo is on schedule," Stone said.

They were a good team, and that's what made them as successful as they were. Stone was brilliant with demolition and the final touches. Hunter's skill was everything in the middle. He loved his job, but he had to admit, it wouldn't take a lot of convincing to give up the long hours and tough physical labor. Something that wasn't happening before Thanksgiving.

He wouldn't be skipping this year either. His mother had gone to great lengths to pull a promise from him, and he wouldn't let her down. Which meant twelve-hour days were in his future. That was the only way he could see this house finished by the time he left.

Hunter checked his progress on the tile and sighed. "Yeah, I guess I'll clean up here and call it a day. It's not long before the sun sets."

Stone left, and Ryan took his spot in the doorway.

"I'm thinking you have questions for me," said Hunter.

Ryan waited a beat, seeming unsure if he should ask the question. "I was wondering if I could maybe talk to you sometime about how you got into flipping houses. That is, if you don't mind."

Chuckling, Hunter began tucking his tools into the bucket he used to keep them together. He had a larger toolbox, but the bucket with pouches on the side worked much better for him on the job site. "No, I wouldn't mind."

"Awesome. Thanks. I'll see you tomorrow," Ryan said and gave a two-finger salute as he left.

Once Hunter was sure he had all his tools, he took a quick tour of the house and then locked up. Before getting into his pickup, he set the tool bucket on the floor behind the driver's seat. One of the first things he'd tell Ryan was that leaving tools out was a surefire way to lose them to a five-finger discount. Keeping his tools safe would save him countless hours of frustration.

He climbed into his truck and paused for a moment, enjoying the comfort of sitting. Yeah, it was a long, hot shower kind of night. He sighed, starting his vehicle and backing out of the driveway. The sun was just barely peeking over the horizon. It had been another long day.

On the way to his hotel a little farther inland, his thoughts drifted to the picturesque seaside bed and breakfast. When he'd first arrived on the island, he'd missed the cute little place on his drive to one of the worksites. That evening he'd noticed it, though, it had been like a lighthouse, drawing him in.

He'd stopped by, and the owner had assumed he was a guest spending the night. Instead of correcting her, he'd happily followed her all over the home. It had been a little awkward when she'd found out after, but it had been worth whatever lame excuse he'd thrown out at the time.

From what he'd learned, the last big hurricane had really beaten the place up. The paint was peeling. The wraparound porch needed some new boards. In his head, he'd made a list of things to fix inside and tallied the bill. He'd felt it was worth every penny to enjoy the little slice of heaven it would offer.

Not only had the property made an impression on him that day but also the owner, Reagan Loveless. Man, even now he could still remember the shocked look on her face when he'd made an off-the-cuff offer to buy the place after stopping in a few times. It had been the wrong move, even after waiting a while to inquire, and he'd known it the moment her shock turned to anger. The petite woman had pulled back her shoulders, crossed her arms over her chest, and told him it would never be for sale. It had been in her family for decades, and it was going to stay that way.

Since that night, neither the bed and breakfast nor Reagan had been far from his thoughts. Not only was the property appealing, but she was too. Blonde hair that touched the tops of her shoulders, fiery dark eyes. She was the very definition of perfection when it came to Hunter's ideal woman. Not only was she beautiful, but she had the brain to go with it.

If only he were in the market for a girlfriend, but it wasn't the right time. Other than money, he didn't have anything to offer a woman yet. He was still working long days, and his attention was on his business. No, he didn't have to work, but he wanted to. He'd worked hard to build the company with Stone. Hunter wasn't quite ready to give it up.

As The Sandy Pelican came into view, he slowed to a stop. A single light cast a glow through the window onto the railing. Reagan was working in the office which was near the kitchen. In a split-second decision, which he'd probably regret later, he turned off the road onto the winding driveway leading to the front of the house, parked, and walked to the steps.

Hopefully, he wasn't intruding, but this place spoke to him. Hunter couldn't put a finger on why, but it felt like home to him. He could see a future with a wife and kids. Not that he thought he was ready for all that, but it didn't shake the idea of what could be.

That's if he could somehow convince the stubborn owner to sell it to him. Maybe if he shared his vision with Reagan, she'd be more amiable to letting it go. He didn't want to tear it down and build a strip mall. His plan was to just update it a little. Maybe put a porch swing up so he could drink his coffee and watch the sunrise of a morning.

He got out of his pickup, slowly making his way to the bottom of the steps. "I could do so much with you." He laid his hand on the worn step railing. With a little love, he could bring the old home back to its former glory.

Of course, the only response was a soft breeze. In the distance, he could hear the waves crashing and the whisper-like foam soaking into the sand.

He sighed and continued up the steps. He was hoping for the best and preparing for a firm no. With luck, that's all he'd get. Then again, he was at least a foot taller than Reagan. Unless she was pretty flexible, his backside was safe from her small foot.

CHAPTER 2

For the first time all day, Reagan Loveless parked herself in the office chair as the sun slipped below the horizon. Her shoulders slumped as she leaned over her desk, weariness seeping deep into her bones. Words like tired and exhausted came to mind along with ten other adjectives to describe how she felt. Not the typical attributes of a thirty-year-old woman, but that's what happened when the real world called...collect. Could she continue going? Maybe, but right then, sitting alone in the tiny office in the back of the bed and breakfast, she wasn't so sure.

It didn't really matter if she could or not. Even if she did have a choice, giving up wasn't an option. She had reservations, however meager, that she had to honor. That meant her rinse-and-repeat life would continue the same way it had since she'd taken over The Sandy Pelican two years ago. It wasn't like the tower of bills would magically pay themselves.

No, Reagan's only choice was to do whatever it took to keep the bed and breakfast afloat. No matter how hopeless she felt. She sighed and picked up the envelope with her bank's return address. The one that held her loan. Even without opening it, she knew it wasn't good news.

Before she could tear open the envelope, her phone rang, breaking the eerie silence and startling her. She held in a groan. Her little sister, Carlin. She quickly pulled her short hair back and tucked it into a clip before answering. "Hey, sis."

"Hey." It wasn't the word as much as how it was said. Not really condescending, but not exactly thrilled either.

Her sister ran a high-end clothing boutique in Atlanta. It wasn't that Carlin tried to be better at everything she did; it just came naturally. For once, Reagan wanted to be good at something too. She was tired of being the failure of the family.

"What's going on?" Reagan asked.

"I was about to ask you that." Carlin paused. "Mom and Dad said something about you struggling."

At least Reagan hadn't opened the bank's letter yet. This way she wouldn't be lying. "I'm struggling, but this is the slow season. There aren't a lot of people who plan beach getaways when the water is so cold the waves are made of ice cubes."

Carlin sighed. "I know, but if you're struggling now, how will you make it to tourist season?"

Reagan set her elbow on the desk and her chin in her hand. "The same way Mom and Dad made it each year. A wing and a prayer."

Her parents had signed over The Sandy Pelican when they retired. At the time, Reagan hadn't even considered that anything would change. The first couple of years were pretty good. Tourism was up, the island was seeing explosive growth, and it was a popular destination for weddings and honeymoons. One article had called it a charming Southern slice of life.

The most her parents had ever encountered were a couple of bad storms, but they'd fixed the place afterward. It wasn't until the property was hers that she realized they'd been seeing a downturn in reservations. According to some guests, they liked the bed and breakfast, but it needed updating.

"Sounds like you need a flock of wings and more than a few prayers."

"This is how things are. It'll bounce back. I just need to ride it out." Reagan worked to keep any emotion out of her voice.

Then the last hurricane had roared onto shore, and nothing had gone right since. The entire house was a money pit at this point. She'd taken out a large equity loan to fix the damage done by the storm, but there'd been even bigger issues with the roof than a few missing shingles. Then they'd found an issue with the pipes under the house. She'd bled green, even going so far as to max out her credit cards. It was as if she were cursed by an evil leprechaun. Instead of a pot of gold at the end of the rainbow, the little jerk was digging in her pockets and kicking her in the shins when he didn't find anything.

"Do you really think you'll be able to do that?" Carlin asked.

"I think so." This time Reagan couldn't keep the small tremble out of her voice. "I'm really trying."

Carlin sighed. "I know you are, and I'm not trying to be a bearer of bad news or beat you up. I know how you get, though. You're stubborn, and you don't know when to call it quits."

Reagan sat back in her chair, running a piece of thread sticking out from her shirt through her fingers. She picked up the bank letter again and ripped it open.

She needed to face the piper while her sister was on the phone. Her entire body sagged. "It's a foreclosure notice."

Carlin gasped. "Oh, Reagan. Maybe it's time to—"

"No. These things take time, and I will find a way to come up with the money. I'm not giving up on this place. I'll chain myself to something before I let them take it." Boy, it sounded so good that even Reagan believed the short burst of bravado.

"Do you think you can? Where are you going to get enough money to make the loan current and keep up the payments? Mom and Dad said the place still needs a ton of work."

"I know it does."

"And do you really want to sink every dime you have into it when you know..." She paused a beat. "When you know you may not be able to keep it?"

Carlin was talking like there were more dimes to sink into it. Reagan nearly snorted and said, "As if." But she held the snarky comment back. Instead, she took a deep breath as reality settled in.

Tears pooled in the corner of Reagan's eyes. "I just can't give up."

"Reagan, I know you've always felt like..." It seemed like she was searching for the best word.

"A failure because you're good at everything?"

Carlin groaned. "You aren't a failure. You're the hardest working person I know. Whether the bed and breakfast succeeds or not, it won't be your fault. You've put your heart and soul into it."

Reagan sniffed. She could have some knock-down, drag-outs with her sister, but she was also the best at wiping away tears. "Do you really think that?"

"I don't think it; I know it. If there's a way to save that place, you're the only one I'd trust to do it."

The little confidence booster her sister was dishing out was making her feel better. It didn't change her circumstances, but sometimes just knowing someone believed in you was enough to revive a fighting spirit. "Thanks, Carlin."

"I love you, Reagan. I just...I want you to be happy."

"I love you too. I want the same for you." Reagan needed a mental break from her problems, if only for a minute. "That reminds me. How did that date go the other night?"

The arrogant house flipper, Hunter, floated to mind. Sheesh. That guy. At first, she'd thought he was downright adorable. Little dimple on his left cheek. That flashy smile. And, mercy, those blue eyes. Those things were like beacons. He'd been by more than a dozen times before she knew his real motive for coming by. Man, he was charming. She'd been close to picking out china when he'd offered to buy her family's bed and breakfast.

Oh, he'd made her furious. All that charm to butter her up into selling. She'd told him under no uncertain terms was she selling. Then he'd had the audacity to tell her he knew it was in financial trouble.

All her life, she'd thought Southern men knew better than to kick a wasp's nest. Clearly, Hunter West had missed that school tutorial, but, buddy, she'd gotten him up to speed real fast. She'd been so ticked that she'd knocked back enough sleepy tea to put an elephant down. Just thinking about it got her dander up.

"What are you mumbling about, sis?" Carlin asked her.

Reagan startled. "What?"

"You said something about wasps and elephants. I'm not entirely sure how those two things relate to one another."

"Oh, nothing. Sorry. My thoughts drifted for a second. Now, tell me about that date."

Reagan could imagine her sister hunkering down to give the whole scoop. More than likely, not only would Carlin be better at business, she'd be a pro at relationships too. Her little sister was young, cute, and way more popular in high school than Reagan could have ever thought of being.

More than once, Carlin had chastised Reagan for focusing on her failures rather than her successes. Only, Carlin didn't understand. Her business was thriving. She was doing well. It was easier not to compare when everything was perfect.

As Reagan listened to her sister, she sent up a silent prayer in the hopes that maybe someone or something was listening. All she wanted was to taste a little success. It didn't even have to be perfect success. Just… a nibble. The cookie could be hard on the top and burned on the bottom. She wasn't asking for much. Just a small jaunt through that bright green plush grass that seemed to always stay on the other side of the fence.

CHAPTER 3

Hunter had knocked a few times, and then he'd figured Reagan hadn't heard him, so he let himself in. He'd stepped into the kitchen quietly then heard her say, "It's a foreclosure notice."

It bugged him that he felt like a vulture circling in wait for the place to take its last breath. He hated how dire her situation was, but he'd learned early on that making things personal only led to complications. This was just business. If he didn't buy it, someone else would. Who could say they wouldn't tear it to the ground and put up a beachfront condo? At least he wasn't doing that.

When he realized she was having a private conversation, he'd quietly stepped back out. There was no reason to let her know he'd overheard her conversation and embarrass her. He might be a shrewd businessman, but he was also a gentleman.

While he waited for her to finish her phone call, he put his back to the door, took a deep breath, and let the salty breeze wash over him. This was peace. All he needed was some sweet tea, a warm woman, and a swing, and this would be his definition of paradise.

As he shifted his weight from one foot to the other, a board creaked. Another thing he mentally added to the list of things to fix. When he no longer heard the murmur of Reagan's voice, he paused a minute and then knocked again.

"Hello?" Reagan said as she opened the door. A second later, the yellow glow of a porch light flickered to life.

He blinked as his eyes adjusted. "Hey, Reagan."

"Hunter." The sharp tone held a warning that he needed to tread carefully.

Just as he thought she was going to slam the door in his face, she took a deep breath and said, "Come in."

As he entered the kitchen, it wasn't a shock that it was spotless, and he knew she'd cooked for the handful of guests staying there. So far, all the gossip about Reagan had been true, which meant she'd been the cook for years. That didn't necessarily translate to business savvy. He'd learned long ago that it took more than talent alone to make a company successful.

Hunter's first year partnering with Stone was filled with mistakes. It was easy to get behind on bills and then realize the funds were barely there to pay them. For that reason alone, he sympathized with Reagan's situation, but that didn't change his mind about wanting the place.

His mother would be devastated that he'd be living so far away from Caprock Canyon. Her vision of grandchildren running around wasn't a secret, but she'd also taught him that independence was a virtue. While she'd understand, he'd be getting plenty of visits, especially when he started having children.

Reagan crossed her arms over her chest as she stood in the middle of the kitchen. "The place still isn't for sale."

No beating around the bush with her. "I was hoping we could talk."

With a large sigh, she dropped her arms to her sides. "Fine. Can I offer you something to drink? Some tea or coffee?" It was as if the small offer had pained her. Had he been that big of a jerk last time?

Well, from her perspective, he suspected he was. "No, thanks. This isn't a social visit."

"I know, but I *do* have manners." She motioned to

the table and mismatched chairs nestled in the large bay window. "Sit."

He followed her, but instead of taking a seat, he braced his hands on the back of one of them, and she mirrored him. For a second, he hesitated to park himself because he wasn't sure he could get back up. Tight deadlines and hard work were taking their toll on him. Finally, he took a seat, thinking that if he were in her shoes and someone of his stature was towering over him, he'd feel intimidated, and that wasn't how he wanted her to see him.

"I appreciate the offer, but I don't need anything." His mother had taught him manners too. "I know the place isn't officially for sale, but everyone has a price."

She took in a ragged breath, her shoulders lifting then slumping. "Well, I don't, and if you keep pestering me, I won't let you inside anymore."

Where had that come from? "Pestering you? This is only the second conversation we've had about selling the place."

"It's two times too many," she said, catching his gaze and holding it.

The fierce determination in her eyes with the tiny lift of her chin held a challenge. It was brief, but the thought floated through his mind that he wished she'd look at him like she was glad to see him. What would it be like if he was the source of her happiness? Just as quickly as the notion hit, he pushed it away. He dealt in facts, not fantasy. There wasn't room in his life for a woman, and he certainly didn't have time to deal with a woman as stubborn as her.

"You could at least listen to the offer. Do you really want to chance losing the property and finding out the new owner wants to level it for a condo project? I can promise you I will not tear it down."

As she studied him, he wondered what she could be thinking. She had to know her chance of being able to keep it open was slim. Unless she possessed a magic wand, the foreclosure was a sure thing.

Reagan slowly sat across from him. "Why do you want this place so badly?"

Sharing his reasons with a stranger when he hadn't even mentioned it to his business partner seemed like a bad move. It wasn't just his life it would affect, and Stone needed to be the first one to know. "Why do you need to know that?"

Shrugging, she said, "Because I'm curious. If I were to sell—and I'm not—I think I have a right to know." She looked around the kitchen and then back at him. "Wouldn't you want to know if you were in my shoes?"

"If it were me, I'd figure maybe they have their reasons and don't want to share them with someone they don't even know." For the tiniest second, he wondered if she'd been playing hardball with him because she knew about his money, but he'd been extra careful about hiding his wealth. He wanted to be known for who he was and not what he had.

She cocked her head. "I grew up in this house. If anyone deserves to know what the person is planning, it's me."

If she could be unrelenting, so could he. "I could just wait it out."

"That could take years."

"Not if the bank forecloses." Hunter wanted to throttle himself. Why had he said that?

Oh man. With one scathing stare, he knew he'd messed up. In classic Southern-woman fashion, she leaned back, cocked an eyebrow, and pinched her lips together. There wasn't a man alive that didn't know what that meant. This woman was about to chew him down one side and then the other. And if he were a kid, after she got done, he'd be picking a switch from a tree.

"*How* do you know about that?" Sheesh, enunciating each word. Good heavens, he was glad she wasn't a skunk. Otherwise, he'd be taking a late-night dip in tomato juice. "You were eavesdropping?"

Little warnings clanged in his head. He needed to

choose his words wisely at this point. "It's not what you think. The back door was unlocked, and I didn't think you'd heard me. I stepped in, but as soon as I realized you were on the phone, I stepped back outside."

"But you heard me mention foreclosure." There was no way to miss the anger in her tone. If he wasn't looking to sell off his part of the business, he'd be offering her a job with as formidable as she was. Anyone who underestimated her would regret it.

"I did, and I'm sorry."

The apology did nothing to ease the tension hanging between them. "So you think you have me at a disadvantage?" The iciness in her tone nearly made him scoot his chair back.

"Absolutely not. I think you are an intelligent woman, which is why I don't think you'd just let the bank foreclose on you. I can tell you love this bed and breakfast. That tells me you want control over who purchases it. The only way to do that is to sell it before it's forcibly taken from you." He raked his hand through his hair. "Is there an offer already on the table that I'm unaware of?" It hadn't hit him until right that moment that it was possible he'd been beaten to the table.

"And if I did, why would I tell you that?" She seemed to soften just a hair.

"Because I can beat it. Just tell me what it is."

"Maybe I don't want to tell you. If I told you, you'd only offer a little bit more." The cool expression on her face didn't change, and he was too tired to play poker. Plus, if he wasn't sharing his reasons for wanting the bed and breakfast, she didn't have to share her reasons for keeping him in the dark. "This way, you have no idea the dollar amount I'm considering. It means you'll have to go whole hog or walk away."

Hunter was rendered momentarily speechless. Awkward silence blanketed the room until his knee began to bounce. *Did* she know about his money? Aside from just wanting to keep her home, it could be an excellent explanation for her stubborn desire to hang on to the place when she knew her chances for keeping it were slim.

He pushed the thought away. No one on Tybee Island had any idea he had money, and there was no reason for anyone to think that he did. Would a billionaire still be part owner of a flipping business? "Look, if there's an offer, just tell me. Playing hard to get is tiring."

Again, he'd put his foot in his mouth.

She stood, walked to the door, and opened it. "I think it's time for you to go."

Yep, this conversation had so many forks in it, it could be used to strain water. He slowly rose from the chair and closed the distance between them. "You have my card. When you're ready to tell me the other offer so I can counter, call me."

After leaving her in the kitchen, he climbed into his truck and waited for her to turn off the porch light. When it stayed on, he pictured her tiny frame hunched over a desk, wondering how she was going to keep it together. His chest constricted, knowing it had to be hard. Someone with her strong will wouldn't go down without a fight. If she didn't have his respect before, she'd definitely earned it tonight.

With one swift motion, he started his truck and put it in gear. He'd barely made it to the end of the driveway when his phone rang. He checked his caller ID. His mother. He couldn't not answer. If he did, she'd just track him down through Stone.

He stopped the truck and turned it off as he hit the call button. "Hi, Mom." Hopefully, she was only calling to verify he was coming home for the holidays.

Since buying the ranch in Caprock Canyon, Bear had gone full-tilt into getting it running again, starting with the farmhouse. The previous year, the whole family had stayed together through the holidays, from Thanksgiving to New Year's, as they prepared for his sister, Carrie Anne, to get married on New Year's Eve. Not only did his sister get married, but his youngest brother had proposed to Gabby Fredericks, their good family friend.

It had put a highlight on just how lonely Hunter felt and was the catalyst that had him thinking it was time to slow down, retire, and have a family. If his youngest brother could find happiness, Hunter could too.

"Hey, sweetheart, you sound tired," his mom said.

With the mention of the word, he yawned. "I am."

She sighed long and loud. "I'm worried about you, Hunter. You're working too hard."

That was an understatement. "I know. I'll take a break soon. What did you need, Mom?"

"It can wait."

"No, go ahead."

She waited a beat. "I just want to make sure your fiancée is coming with you to Thanksgiving."

He squeezed his eyes closed. Oh, crud. Earlier in the year, his sister had threatened to post him on a matchmaking website—the same one she'd put his brother Bear on, which meant it was a threat he couldn't ignore. He'd blurted out that he was engaged, and it had traveled through the grapevine as fast as a gasoline fire. Throughout the year, he'd continued letting them believe the lie since it got them off his back. Now it was about to take a chunk out of his hide. "Uh..."

"Don't you tell me she's too busy this time. If she cares about you at all, she'll be more than happy to meet us."

Hunter peeked upward and silently sent up a prayer. What was he going to do? He searched for an argument that wouldn't make his non-existent fiancée sound like a jerk. "Uh..."

"We don't even know what she looks like. Honey, we just...we love you, and we want to love her too."

At least he'd been smart enough to dodge specifics like her name and what she looked like. Anytime they'd asked, his cell reception had conveniently gone spotty or a catastrophe called for his immediate attention. Only, the vice was getting a little too tight, and if he didn't produce a fiancée this time, his sister would have him on a dozen matchmaker websites before he could blink. What had he gotten himself into?

"Uh...I'll make sure she's there this year." His eyes widened as the words tumbled off his tongue. He was entirely too tired to be talking to his mom; otherwise, he'd have just told her they broke up. "I meant—"

"That's fantastic. I'm so excited to meet her." He could hear the smile in his mom's voice. "Better book your flights pretty quick if you want to sit together. If you waste too much time, you may have to drive."

Hunter blew out a puff of air. "Sure, Mom. But don't worry about picking me up. We'll drive in. Okay?'

"That's reasonable. Don't want to overwhelm her in the middle of an airport. Tell her we're thrilled she's coming. I simply can't wait to meet her."

"I'll tell her."

"Okay, I'll stop running your ear off. Get some rest."

"I will, Mom. Love you."

"Love you too, Hunter."

He ended the call and leaned his head on the steering wheel. Then he remembered where he was. There was no telling what Reagan could be thinking if she'd been watching him drive away, only to see him stop at the end. Knowing her, he was plotting to steal her beachfront.

What had he been thinking? A fiancée? This was totally different than stealing cookies and swearing that Cookie Monster did it. This was a whole person he had to produce out of thin air.

"I am an idiot," he said aloud.

There were zero prospects. The little bit he'd dated didn't give him many options. Most wouldn't even consider pretending to be his significant other. He certainly couldn't rope anyone in Caprock Canyon into doing it. His mother knew everyone, and there was no way they'd have kept it from her.

Just as he lifted his head, the answer hit him. Reagan. The porch light was still on and so was the light in the office. What would she think of him asking her to be his pretend fiancée? Especially after he'd ticked her off. Not only was he a jerk, but he was certifiable too.

More than likely, she'd send him packing, which meant…there was nothing to lose but his pride. Yeah, he was especially eager to stay off those dating websites his sister threatened to put him on, but it was more than that. He didn't want to seem like a failure in the one area of life that mattered. Home and family. More than anything, he wanted his family to be proud of him. He wanted that above all. Even if it meant losing the chance to buy the property of his dreams.

CHAPTER 4

Three times. *Three times* Reagan had checked her front driveway to find Hunter's truck still parked there. He'd said he'd wait her out, but this wasn't what she'd pictured. What was he going to do? Sleep in his truck? She sighed. Her heart was still in the fight, but her body and soul were tired. Giving up was the last thing she wanted to do, but what else was there?

Again, she checked his truck, and he was gone. Then a knock came from the back door. Surely he wasn't up for another round of arguing. She trudged to the back screen door and stopped.

"Hey." He looked about as thrilled to see her as she was him.

"Hunter, it's late. I'm tired, and I have to be up early

to cook breakfast. If this is you looking for round two, I'm gonna have to pass."

His shoulders slumped a little. "Well, I've found myself in a pretty deep hole, and I'm hoping you'll help me climb out."

Reagan regarded him a minute. "Why would I do that?"

He took a long, deep breath, and as he exhaled, she saw in him the same bone-deep weariness she was feeling. Stuffing his hands in his jean pockets, he asked, "Can I come in? Please?"

Despite wanting to shut the door in his face, she found herself more interested in what he could possibly want to talk about. She pushed the door open. "Come on."

He stepped inside, staying close to the door. Whatever had happened between the last time she'd spoken to him and now, it had sucked a little bit of his fight out. Tired lines creased around his eyes and lips. She almost found herself wanting to comfort him, but he was the enemy. Letting down her guard would only give him the ammunition he needed to take her home and business away.

"I really don't want to fight with you," he said softly.

"Then stop...stop hounding me." If she could see he

was tired, surely he could see the same in her. Couldn't he offer just a smidge of mercy just once? She didn't have the energy to fight a war on two fronts: him and the bank.

He held up his hands in surrender. "I'm not the enemy. I don't want to see someone buy it and tear it down."

Leaning her hip on the countertop next to the fridge, she crossed her arms over her chest and her feet at the ankles. "You really think you're the answer to what this place needs?"

"Structurally, the place is sound, but it does need a lot of work. The porch has several boards that need to be replaced. It needs to be painted..." He stopped short and closed his eyes. "That's not why I'm here, though." His chest heaved as he inhaled deeply.

"Sure sounds like it," she snapped. "Is this just another one of your ways to gain my trust because I *don't* trust you?" It was just like rich people to work the sad eyes, make you think they cared, and, *wham,* you're shoved out onto the street.

"No, I'm tired and out of tactics. If I had a white flag, I'd be waving it."

She scoffed. "Then what do you want from me?

"I have...I have a proposition for you. One that will get both of us out of a bind." The swagger he'd walked in with earlier was gone. Either she was letting him get to her or maybe he was backing up. She'd even say he looked a little defeated.

She chewed her bottom lip. "A proposition? What does that mean?"

"Just hear me out. Like I said, I think it'll solve both our problems." He glanced at the table. "Any chance you'd let me sit down again?"

She hesitated and then waved him toward it. "Sure."

He slowly walked to the same chair he'd used before and sat, his shoulders slumped forward just a fraction. Unlike last time when it seemed like he was ready to take on a bear.

Trying to figure him out was much like putting a puzzle of the sky together. Just when she thought she had the right piece, it didn't fit.

She crossed the room and sat across from him. "All right. I'll hear you out, but you've got a tall mountain to climb."

Scrubbing his face with his hands, he set both elbows on the table and held his head. "I know. I doubt you'll even agree to it, but…and I hate to admit this, but I'm a little desperate." The last word came out just above a whisper.

This guy wasn't used to feeling like this. His rough,

calloused hands spoke of hard work, determination, and a man who finished what he started. It earned a little respect from her, but just a little.

"Okay, my interest is definitely piqued now." She scooted down in the chair and put her feet on the seat of another, crossing her feet at the ankles. "What is it that you think I won't agree to?"

He lifted his head and set his arms on the table. "I have a decent-size family. There are four brothers and a sister. We're all fairly close, and after my sister got married last year on New Year's Eve, she decided to make it her mission to get us married off."

A tiny bark of laughter bubbled out. She couldn't have heard that right. "What?"

He touched his hand to his forehead, exhaling sharply. "Why am I even doing this?" He started to get up, and Reagan quickly straightened and grabbed his hand, stopping him.

Tingles of electricity raced up her arm so quickly that she shivered and yanked her hand back. "I'm sorry. I just didn't expect you to say that."

He caught her gaze and held it. Whatever anger she'd harbored toward him earlier had turned to mist and floated away. Hunter was hurting, and if there was one thing she understood, it was hurt. "All right, spill it. I'm guessing it's a bit of a problem with the way you're acting."

His gaze dipped to the floor. "I told my sister I was engaged earlier this year. I didn't want her meddling or trying to fix me up. It just slipped out, and before I knew it, it was this giant lie that I didn't know how to fix."

"Okay, but what does that have to do with me? Or were you just needing someone to talk to?"

This time when he caught her gaze, she felt the shift in his mood. "I need a fiancée. If you will agree to accompany me home for Thanksgiving, pretending we're engaged, I will give you the money to bring your mortgage current, along with the other vendors you're late paying. I'll also throw in a new roof and new porch."

Did he just say what she thought he said? Pretend to be his fiancée? "Are there cameras somewhere? Are you punking me?"

His entire body seemed to slump forward. "I wish I was, but no. It's just for the weekend. When we get back, I will tell them in a few weeks that we broke up. You'll never have to see them again."

"You can't find any ex-girlfriend or woman at home that will be willing to go through with a charade like this?"

Shaking his head, Hunter said, "No, I honestly haven't had that many girlfriends. I've been working since I could pick up a hammer. My schedule and my life don't exactly work for a relationship. And my mom knows all the girls back home. If I'd been engaged to one of them, she'd know it."

"So you need someone your family has never met."

"That's about the gist of it."

She raised an eyebrow. "How is this going to help you get my property? If I take the money and get ahead, I'll never sell."

"This isn't about finding a way to get your property. I would rather you have a way to keep it than to see someone else destroy it. At least this way the place is preserved, even if it isn't mine."

Reagan didn't know what to think. She'd been asked a lot of things, but being someone's fake fiancée had never been on her radar. "I don't know..."

Hunter nodded. "I figured you would need to think about it. I know if the roles were reversed, I'd have to do some hardcore mulling myself."

"That's an understatement. You're asking me to help you lie to your family. Are you sure that's something you want to do?"

The lines around his eyes and lips deepened, and he hung his head. "Not really, but," he exhaled heavily,

"I don't want to meet someone on the internet either. I have no problems with them or people wanting to use dating sites. I just don't want that."

She took her lower lip in her teeth. The vibe she was getting from him was that this wasn't his normal way of doing things. "Would it just be easier to come clean? If they love you, they'll understand."

"I really don't want to disappoint my mom." He mumbled something, and she couldn't be sure she heard him right, but she could've sworn he'd tacked on "as always" at the end. This man didn't strike her as someone who let people down often.

Before he'd offered to buy her bed and breakfast, she'd been really attracted to him, going even so far as to be a bumbling mess around him. It wouldn't be a real chore to call him fiancée. Still, lying to an entire group of people and keeping up the pretense that they were together? That could be a spider's web of lies to get tangled up in. Was it worth it?

"I really need to think about it," Reagan said.

He lifted his head, and the blue eyes that had captivated her the first time she met him were filled with sorrow. "I know. I'm not going to rush you. Thanksgiving is in two weeks, and you have until then." He slowly stood and rubbed his hands down his jeans. "I'll get going. I have an early morning, and I bet you do too."

She rose from her chair and walked with him to the door. "Well, breakfast isn't going to cook itself."

"I sometimes wish these houses would remodel themselves," he said with a chuckle. "You've got my number, right?"

"Yeah, I still have your card from the last time you were here."

Once he was out the door, she shut and locked it. Leaning against it, she went back over their conversation. It sure was a lot to consider. A relationship itself was hard enough without pretending to be in one. Still, the prospects of getting current on her note along with the roof and porch fixed sure was tempting. What other options did she have?

She covered her mouth with her hand as she yawned. It was also something she needed to ponder when she wasn't feeling like the walking dead. This was a decision for after her morning coffee tomorrow.

CHAPTER 5

If there was a record for checking a person's phone, Hunter would be a gold champion. Since his conversation with Reagan a week ago, he'd been glued to his phone, waiting for her to call with her answer. If this was payback for offering to purchase The Sandy Pelican, it was working.

"You've been looking at your phone every ten minutes for days now. Do you have a girlfriend I don't know about?" Stone asked, holding a cabinet ready for installation.

Not hardly, but Hunter didn't want to share the real reason either. The amount of ribbing he'd get wasn't worth it. Instead of answering his partner, he tucked his phone back in his jean pocket and changed the subject. “Did the new dumpster get delivered to the other job site?”

The one that had originally been delivered had filled up quickly from the demolition. They’d underestimated what they’d needed, and demo had stopped for a few days until the dumpster company could get them a bigger one.

His partner shook his head. “Nice sidestep there, buddy. Yeah, it’s been delivered.”

This was one of the reasons Hunter hated delegating jobs. It was too easy to get stalled on a project and delay getting it on the market. More often than not, things like that had a domino effect, and it cost them money. Another item on Hunter’s list of cons for the business. It made him that much more motivated to sell his half. Even if he didn’t end up purchasing the bed and breakfast, he was done flipping.

Hunter took the cabinet from Stone and rested it on the piece of wood he’d nailed to the wall as a guide. Stone wouldn’t have needed it. This was where their individual talents came into play. Hunter couldn’t eyeball things like Stone. The guy had a knack for just knowing if something was straight or not. If only that gift carried over to demo. Stone never accounted for unknown issues, even after all these years.

With the cabinet held in place, Hunter used the drill to sink the screw. They'd be hidden once the tile backsplash was installed.

"I guess demo has started again, then?" Hunter asked.

Stone nodded. "Yeah, but it got there late, so we'll only get about an hour before it's quitting time."

Hunter held his frustration in. "Better than none at all."

"You're going to that job site to do some demo after this, aren't you?"

Hunter stepped off the ladder he'd used to reach the top screws and surveyed his work. "I might."

"Let's go out for a beer. I'm going to save you from yourself tonight," Stone said.

Hunter's phone buzzed in his pocket, and he quickly pulled it out. Reagan. He answered and motioned to Stone that he'd be back in a minute. "Hi." He walked out of the kitchen and away from listening ears.

"Hi, Hunter," Reagan said.

It had been years since he'd been this nervous to talk to someone. Then again, it wasn't every day he offered to pay someone to be engaged to him. And when he put it like that, it put a bad taste in his mouth.

"Uh..." She cleared her throat. "Do you happen to be free for dinner at my place tonight?"

Dinner? He blinked. "Uh, sure," he said. Like he'd have plans. Hardly. If he wasn't having dinner with her, he'd be eating pretzels at a sports bar with Stone, watching a game he didn't care about played by people he didn't know. Eating a meal with Reagan would be a step up, even if they just ate pretzels.

"Good. Think you could make it to the bed and breakfast by, say, six or so?"

If he had to cross an ocean, he'd be there. If she was flat-out telling him no, she wouldn't be asking to have dinner. Or she could be offering him dinner to let him down easy. Great, now he'd be riding a mental seesaw until he saw her.

"Yeah, I can do that." He pulled the phone from his ear and checked the time. If he left as soon as the call ended, he could even grab a shower.

"Great. I'll see ya then."

The call ended, and he stared at his phone screen for second and then slipped it back into his pocket.

"You look perplexed," Stone said.

Hunter wheeled around, startled. "Uh, no, I'm good, but I need to get that last cabinet up."

"Yeah, sure." His partner shrugged. "What's the rush, though?"

"I'll have to raincheck the offer for a beer. I had something come up that isn't work-related."

Stone eyed him a moment. They'd learned long ago that if one didn't want to give up information, they didn't press it. "All right, then let's get it done. I'm ready for a ball game and some downtime."

So was Hunter, but with his looming meeting with Reagan, downtime wasn't happening. He wasn't sure what to hope for, but either way, after tonight, he'd at least have an answer. Once he had that, he could plan accordingly.

AFTER PARKING HIS TRUCK, Hunter stepped out as the sun cast an orange glow over everything it touched. With the way the cicadas were chirping, the temperature tomorrow was going to be triple digits with a hundred-percent chance of humidity. Good thing the air conditioning in the project house worked.

As he reached the backdoor to the kitchen, the first thing to hit him was the smell of something delicious wafting through the screen. Man, he hoped she made enough for seconds. He squinted and made out an aproned Reagan holding a bottle of wine while standing in front of the stove. Then he realized she was humming, and he could hear the joy in it. She enjoyed cooking.

She must have heard him because she looked up and said, "Come in."

He stepped inside, and the aroma was even stronger. "Whatever that is, it smells amazing." The second it was out of his mouth, his stomach loudly rumbled. A small part of him hoped she'd not only made enough for seconds, but thirds, and maybe even a takeout box. A little sweet tea was the only thing that could make it better.

Chuckling, she said, "Chicken française. Go ahead and take a seat." She tipped her head toward the table.

"Thanks." He glanced at the table set for two. The lack of candles assured him it would be all business. If he were honest, he wasn't sure what he thought about that. What if they weren't on opposite sides? Having dinner with a beautiful woman sounded pretty good.

"Are you thirsty? I've made some fresh sweet tea."

She must have been reading his mind. "I'd love some."

The smile she flashed him reached her eyes, and he was struck by the brightness of it. He hadn't noticed that before. Then again, anytime he'd come to The Sandy Pelican, it had been on business. Not that this wasn't business, but...he shook the thought away. He was hungry. Clearly, he couldn't think straight at the moment.

"I'm in the middle of this, so please help yourself. The pitcher's in the fridge, and the glasses are in the cabinet to the left of it."

On his way to the table, he helped himself to a tall glass. He took a long drag of the cold perfectly sweetened liquid. He refilled his glass and then poured her a glass as well.

Just as he set their glasses on the table, she poured some wine into the pan, and it flamed up. Considering the ease in which she handled it, it was something that happened fairly regularly. It showed a different side of her. One that was self-assured and confident. It took her from beautiful to downright gorgeous.

After plating their food, she placed one in front of him before taking a seat across from him with her own meal. "Thank you for the drink."

"Sure," he said, staring at the meal in front of him while taking his utensils out of the linen napkin and draping it over his lap.

"Eat. I promise you it's not poisoned."

He lifted his gaze to hers and chuckled. "I hadn't thought of that. Maybe I should wait until you eat it."

She cut a piece of chicken then popped it into her mouth. "See. All okay."

Man, she was so different from the last time they'd spoken...and he liked this side of her. "I suspect it's way better than okay."

He dug into his chicken, swiping it through the sauce and gathering a forkful of rice. As he chewed, it took effort not to pinch himself just to make sure he hadn't died and gone to heaven. He'd never tasted anything so good. After he swallowed, he said, "Wow."

A blanket of pink covered her cheeks. "Thank you."

Not only could she cook, but she was adorable when she blushed. Alarm bells sounded in his head. If she agreed to his proposal, he'd have to take extra steps to keep her at a distance. Too many thoughts like that one, and he'd be in serious trouble.

He set down his fork, determined to keep the conversation professional. "This is flat-out the most delicious thing I've ever eaten. You're really good at this."

She tilted her head, a tiny smile playing on her lips. "You sound surprised."

"Well, no, not really surprised, just...in awe of your talent."

A small laugh bubbled out of her. Okay, not only was the food wow, but so was she. That laugh...and her snuggled next to him, watching the sunset… No, no, no. Business. This was business, nothing else.

She narrowed her eyes, but the smile stayed on her lips. "Don't think that flattery will get me to sell."

"I wouldn't dare." He grinned. Was he flirting with this woman? Have mercy, he was. How long had it been since he'd done that?

Silence, along with the elephant in the room, fell over them as they ate a few bites. Anxiety built in Hunter's chest until he finally put down his fork and asked, "Okay, I need to know. What's your answer?"

"Cut to the chase, huh?"

"Please? If you're letting me down easy, I need to figure out what I'm going to tell my family."

Taking a sip of her tea, she held his gaze as she peered over the rim of the glass. She set it back down and wiped her mouth with the napkin before dropping it back into her lap. "All right. If I'm going to do this, I have additions to the agreement."

He almost said she wasn't in a position to negotiate, but that wasn't exactly true. Plus, if he said that, she'd probably get mad and kick him out. First, he wanted to finish the meal, and second, he didn't want her to say no. If her additions were too outlandish, he'd simply counter with his own. "Okay, what are they?"

"On top of getting me current on the loan, I want a year's worth of payments and enough money to do some of the upgrades I know it needs."

Once again, the thought that she somehow knew about his money came roaring to his mind. Why did she think he had that kind of money? Granted, he did run a flipping business and he'd offered to buy her place. Not just offered, but said he'd beat out any other offer she'd received. For most people, that would make him sound like he either had money or access to it.

"Why not the loan payoff?" he asked.

She shrugged and lowered her eyes to the table. "I'm not looking for the easy way out." She lifted her head and met his gaze. "I want to prove to myself that I can do it. Yes, I could still do that with the loan paid off, but I'd never really know it was me. It's easy to run a business when there's no pressure."

Wow. If he didn't respect her before, he did now. What an incredible woman. She was a dangerous combination of beautiful, charming, and intelligent. The type of woman he'd secretly wanted for a while now. The level of risk for him had rocketed in the span of a few sentences.

Then again, he also knew it would be difficult to lure tourists back when their last visit wasn't so great. She was a fighter, but you could only keep it up for so long. If she invested the capital back into the place, it would only make it easier on him later on when he purchased it. He wasn't being cruel, just pragmatic.

He held her gaze a second longer and said, "If I agree to your terms, you'll pretend to be my fiancée?"

"Yes, but I'm still wondering why you picked me."

"I..." What should he say? Yes, his mother knew all the women back in Caprock Canyon. Maybe there was even a possibility he could have asked one of his exes, but deep down, the truth was that he liked her. She was the type of woman he'd bring home to his mom.

"What?" Reagan asked.

"My mom knows everyone back home, and..."

"I was the nearest available?"

The hint of sadness in her voice made him pause. He ate a few more bites of his meal as he worked to form a response. She had to know she was incredible. Not only was she an amazing cook, but she was easy—and fun—to talk to. "No, well, yes, but that's not the reason. You're intelligent, witty, and beautiful. Even if I had choices, I'd have still asked you."

"Well, I didn't expect that answer, but...thank you."

Had no one ever told her that? Shame. Hunter didn't want a relationship, but he certainly wasn't blind. "I find it very difficult to believe no one has ever said that before."

She cleared her throat and nodded. "Okay. You said last time that your family is close." It wasn't lost on him that she'd changed the subject. One more thing to add to the list of things he liked about her.

"Yeah, we are." He took a deep breath. "I'll be upfront. This isn't going to be easy to pull off."

Her eyebrows hit her hairline. "Are you trying to talk me out of it?"

Shaking his head, he said, "No, but I want you to know what you're agreeing to. I don't want you blind-sided when we get there."

"Fair enough. There's one more thing I want."

"What's that?" he asked, eyeing her.

"I want everything in writing. That way we both know what is expected of the other." She took a bite of food and washed it down with some tea.

While he mulled it over, he finished the last few bites of his meal. "That's fair. I'll need to know what will get you current, the tally of a year's worth of payments, and estimates on the upgrades."

"I'll get the number together, and you'll have them in the next twenty-four hours."

"That's not much time to get estimates," he replied.

She smiled. "I know what things need to be fixed.

Before the hurricane hit, my plan for the equity loan was to fix those things."

"Then these estimates are a year old. They're no good now."

With a huff, she stood, grabbed their empty plates, and deposited them in the sink. On her way back to the table, she stopped at the fridge and fished out a pie. "I know, but I figure if I add fifteen percent to them, that'll account for the storm damage or inflation."

She cut into the pie, and his mouth watered. Chocolate cream pie? Either she was asking around about him, or she was psychic. She slid a plated slice toward him. "Hope you like chocolate cream."

"Like it? It's my favorite."

The cute smile she'd flashed him earlier returned. "Good." Once she'd plated her own slice, she took her seat again. "It's tied as my favorite. I love coconut cream too."

Just how much in common did he have with her? "Me too."

"Really?"

"Yeah, but then again, I've never met a pie I didn't like." He smiled sheepishly.

A giggle popped out of her, and she scooped a bite of pie into her mouth.

Man, she was irresistible. If the alarm bells hadn't

gone off earlier, they'd be wailing now. This woman was checking all his boxes, and they'd hardly spent any time together yet. How was he going to manage several days in a row...while pretending to be her fiancée?

While he contemplated that, he took a bite of the pie and nearly moaned. His mother had just lost first place as best pie maker ever. Not that he'd ever admit that aloud. He wasn't that stupid. "This is incredible."

"Thank you," she said and continued eating.

As he watched her, he reassessed his risk factor. They'd be arriving in Caprock Canyon the day before Thanksgiving and returning that Sunday. That was a total of five days. As long as he kept a comfortable arm's length from her, he'd be just as single when he got back as he was now.

Starting something with Reagan wouldn't be the casual dating he'd done in the past. If he started something with her, it would be with the intent of reaching the finish line with her. And when he'd tried to purchase her home? Starting a relationship was hard enough, but add distrust and it was already doomed. Would she ever believe he wanted to date her?

Why was he even thinking about it? Like she'd even consider dating him in the first place. She saw him as the enemy. He had no problem keeping their relationship right where it was: frenemies.

A small voice in the back of his head quietly laughed as he played a game of chicken. He was pretty sure he was going to lose.

CHAPTER 6

Even though The Sandy Pelican didn't have any reservations for Thanksgiving weekend, that didn't mean that there wouldn't be that lone guest needing a last-minute place to stay. With that in mind, Reagan asked her two best friends to keep it open.

In fifth grade, Kaylee Benson and Naomi Knowles moved to the island with their mom and dad. Their parents had married after they met through a support group for grieving spouses a few years earlier. Since they'd moved to the neighborhood, the three of them had been the three musketeers.

Naturally, they'd asked why Reagan needed them, and she'd dodged the truth until she and her overfilled suitcase were face-to-face with them. If she'd been smart, she would have asked Hunter what she needed to bring instead of stuffing her poor suitcase to the point of bursting.

"What?" Naomi asked after Reagan explained everything.

Kaylee simply blinked.

"I know it's wild, but—"

"Wild? That's not wild. It's…is there even a word for it?"

Putting all her weight on the lid of the suitcase, Reagan forced the zipper around the lid of the bag and sat next to it. "Look, if I thought I had another option, I would have done it."

Kaylee crossed the room and perched on the other side of the suitcase. Of her two friends, Kaylee was the more soft-spoken one. She ran a cat rescue, and both Reagan and Naomi thought she'd needed a break from the stress of the job. This weekend would be perfect for her.

"Isn't he the enemy? Didn't you tell us he's the one trying to swoop in and steal the bed and breakfast from you?" Kaylee asked.

Reagan sighed as she finished. "Yes, but—" She lifted her head and met Naomi's gaze. "I've run out of every penny I have. This wouldn't have been my chosen way to fix things, but what else could I do?"

Just the day before, she'd signed the contract, he'd handed her half of the agreed amount, and she'd promptly taken it to the bank. There had been a heaping dose of satisfaction in taking Hunter's money and getting her equity loan current.

"There had to be a better way."

Reagan's shoulders sagged. "I didn't see one."

"What if this guy is a serial killer?"

Sighing, Reagan rolled her eyes. "With the way he talked about his family, there's no way. I know I've told you guys he's a pest, but he's..." After having dinner with him a few nights ago, she'd found herself enjoying his company. Aside from being trip-over-yourself gorgeous, he had an incredible laugh.

"Oh my gosh. You like him!" Naomi blurted.

"I do not. He's a rat who's trying to steal my bed and breakfast. Now I've got the upper hand. Not only is he *not* going to get The Sandy Pelican, but I'm going to use his money to rub his nose in it."

Kaylee smiled. "I think she does."

"Both of you need to—"

A knock came from the back door. Before Reagan could say a word, Naomi shot out of the room with Kaylee following behind.

Reagan pinched the bridge of her nose and groaned. "I should have planned this better." She dropped her hand, hefted her bag off the bed, and pulled it behind her. As she stopped in the kitchen, she found Hunter cornered by Kaylee and Naomi.

"Are you an ax murderer?" Naomi asked Hunter.

Kaylee nudged Naomi with her elbow. "He's too pretty."

Naomi nodded. "True, but he could have had plastic surgery."

Hunter caught Reagan's gaze. "Uh…"

"Hunter, these are my two best friends. The one your left is Kaylee Benson, and the one on your right is Naomi Knowles."

"It's nice to meet you?" Hunter took a step back and smiled. "No, I'm not a…murderer." He touched his face. "Plastic surgery?"

The poor man. Reagan actually felt sorry for him. "Guys, leave him alone."

"We're doing our friend duties and making sure you come back with all your limbs." Naomi shot a look over her shoulder at Reagan with a half-smile and a cocked eyebrow. They'd be talking more once she returned from Texas.

While Naomi was distracted, Hunter slipped past them and crossed the room. As he reached for the handle of her suitcase, his hand brushed against hers.

Little tingles raced through her nerves, sending a shiver down her spine.

He jerked his hand back. "Uh, sorry."

"It's okay. I can handle it."

"If my mom catches you carrying your own luggage, she'll kill me twice." He chuckled, but it had a nervous edge to it. "I'm not saying you aren't capable…"

Reagan smiled and placed her hand on his arm. "It's okay."

A grin slowly lifted his lips. "Did you bring a coat?"

She nodded and patted the outside pocket of her suitcase. "Yeah, I didn't know what to pack, so I brought a little of everything."

"I'm sorry. I should've—"

"Wow," Naomi interrupted. "Witnessing a gentleman in the wild. I almost feel like I need pictures as proof." She chuckled.

Hunter kept his gaze on Reagan. "I'll go get this in the car." Translation: *Your friends are making me uncomfortable.*

"Sure, I'll be out there in a second."

The moment the screen door smacked shut, Reagan's friends were on her like flies on sugar.

"You failed to mention how cute he is," Kaylee said.

Naomi nodded. "No kidding. Please tell me he has single siblings."

Without acknowledging the comments, Reagan hugged one and then the other. "I have to go. We have a flight to catch." She stepped out of the door.

"Call with updates!" Naomi's voice rang out.

Out front, a car waited to take them to the airport. Hunter opened the door for her, and she stepped inside. It was time to get in the fiancée frame of mind.

"Ready?" Hunter asked as he took a seat next to her.

"As ready as I'm going to be."

They were quiet on the drive to the Savannah/Hilton Head airport. He'd mentioned they'd be taking a private jet, and she'd questioned him about it. His response was that he knew someone, but she had a feeling there was more to it. As long as she evaded being body-searched, she'd accept the answer without pushback.

The jet was nice and roomy. It didn't have the rich-snob feel she'd expected. Hunter took a seat across from her, and once it was in the air, he seemed to relax. She wondered if he'd been worried she'd back out.

He cleared his throat. "I guess we should get to know each other. How we met and things like that."

They'd agreed to hash out details of their relationship on the way to Caprock Canyon since it involved both a flight and a two-hour drive. She was glad he was starting the conversation. She'd gone over a million different ways to start that conversation, and none of them sounded right. "We could tell a version of the truth. We met when you stopped by my bed and breakfast. We'll just leave out the part where you tried to steal it from me." She grinned.

Hunter rubbed his jaw with his knuckles as he chuckled. "I'm not trying to steal it from you."

"Okay, maybe steal is a strong word. How about charm it away from me."

A tinge of pink covered his cheeks. "I'd have to possess charm in order to use it."

Whoa. He was cute when he blushed. What caught her off guard was how much she liked it. "We'll say it was love at first sight."

"Me or you?"

"You, of course."

He caught her gaze and held it. "Okay, that won't be hard to sell."

It was her turn to blush. She smiled. "All right. How did you propose?"

"I don't know. You tell me."

She tapped her foot as she contemplated their

story. "Let's see. I love the beach, and since you'd know that, you surprised me with dinner at sunset."

"All right. I'm on board so far." He smiled, and she noticed just how blue his eyes were with the sun filtering in through the window.

"It was very romantic. After dinner, we walked along the beach, and out of nowhere, this puppy came running up to us."

His eyes narrowed. "What kind of puppy?"

"A Great Dane because you know I've always wanted one. His name would be Captain."

He smiled. "Captain?"

"It's the perfect name, and because you're so in love with me, you went along with it."

Hunter nodded and laughed. "Okay. That's actually plausible."

She tilted her head. "Really?"

"I'd really like to have a Great Dane, but I've been too busy."

"Me too," she replied softly, taken aback that they had something in common...besides their favorite pies and their desire to own the bed and breakfast.

He leaned forward, setting his elbows on his knees. "What happened next?"

Reagan's pulse jumped as he stared intently at her. "Uh, well, I scooped up the puppy, and there was a ring hanging on its collar. Then I gasped as you got on one knee and asked me to marry you."

Hunter's gaze dipped to the floor. "That'll be easy to remember." He lifted his head and locked eyes with her. "That sounds like something I'd do."

In that moment, it was so hard to breathe that she half expected the oxygen masks to drop down. It was a fantasy she'd had when she thought about getting engaged. A silly thing because she figured it would never happen that way. Definitely not with the man who wanted to take her family's business. The thought sobered her, and she straightened. "I guess that's good. We won't forget it."

Apparently, he sobered as well because he leaned back. "Yeah, that's good."

A few minutes of silence passed, and Reagan nearly squirmed in her seat. They needed to move to a different topic. "It would probably be a good idea to tell me about your family and Caprock Canyon."

He took a deep breath and looked out the window. While he started filling her in, she worked to keep herself focused. What she needed to remember was that this was all a charade. He could have just said he had things in common with her to get her guard down. Not only that, but what if that's all this was? A clever way to break down her walls and weasel her out of her home.

Well, that wasn't happening, and if he could play this game, so could she. Even if, deep down, she didn't entirely believe it. This was a show and her way of keeping The Sandy Pelican going. Nothing more.

CHAPTER 7

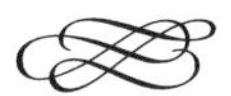

After landing at the Amarillo airport, Hunter and Reagan set out on the two-hour drive to Caprock Canyon in the pickup he'd purchased earlier in the week. Normally, he'd have rented one, but since he knew he'd be returning in a few weeks for Christmas, he figured it would be easier just to pay storage fees and then have one of his brothers drop him off when he left for Georgia again.

The jet, on the other hand, was borrowed. First, he didn't want to own a jet, nor did he want to explain why or how he'd have the ability to own it. As it stood, he'd explained to Reagan that a client had loaned him the use of a private plane.

"Okay, I told you about my family on the way. It's your turn." Hunter shot her a quick glance.

Hopefully, she'd stay away from puppies and proposals. There was a moment on the plane when the air was so sparse, he thought he'd suffocate. She'd started describing the proposal, and with each detail, his heart had thrummed harder. It hadn't been some outlandish, overdone thing. It was simple. Something like what Hunter really would have planned, even down to the breed of dog.

Then the trance was broken, and he'd rattled on about his family, even going so far as to tell her about their good family friends, the Fredericks—Amos, Pauline, Gabby, and Stephanie—and then Bandit, who'd taken one of the ranch hands cabins on Bear's ranch and fixed it up. She'd been quiet the whole time, seemingly soaking in everything he was saying. More than once, he'd caught himself wanting to ask her what she was thinking, but he'd chickened out.

"Well, my parents are full-time RVers, and my sister owns a clothing boutique in Atlanta."

"I wouldn't have guessed that, but it makes sense. I bet they didn't get to travel much when they were running the bed and breakfast."

She smiled. "Yeah, and I understand."

"I hadn't even thought about if you had plans with your family for Thanksgiving." Man, he felt ashamed. He should have at least been a gentleman enough to question her about that before now. He'd been so busy finishing the houses that it hadn't even crossed his mind. "I'm so sorry."

Reagan held up her hand. "It's okay. They're taking a month-long European cruise for their anniversary, and my sister is dating someone. He'd asked her to go with him to meet his family. I'd probably have spent the weekend with Naomi and Kaylee."

"Still, it bugs me that I didn't even consider it. I'm usually...more together than that."

"I don't doubt that. It seems like coming home is a little stressful for you."

Shrugging, Hunter trained his gaze on the road ahead. "A little, but only because I don't want to disappoint them."

"I know that feeling. Things have always been easier for my little sister. Anything she touches is successful, and then you have me. My parents give me the bed and breakfast, and what happens? A hurricane."

Hunter grunted a laugh. "I don't think you had anything to do with the hurricane."

"No, but it sure felt like it."

He didn't miss the sadness in her voice. With the extended close proximity, he'd also become keenly aware of the dark circles around her eyes and how drained she seemed. Before he gave it a second thought, he blurted, "I'm pretty good at fixing floors. Why don't you save the money set aside for that, and when we get back, I'll fix those for you."

She gave him a side-eye. "How much?"

"Nothing."

He took his eyes off the road a second and looked at her. Those mesmerizing, perfect lips of hers were parted, and she blinked. "What?"

"I know you think I'm trying to kick you out of the place, but I'm not. I truly and sincerely don't want it landing in the hands of people who won't appreciate it. It needs a little work, and it'll be perfect."

Reagan looked away, but he thought he caught tears in her eyes. "I'm sorry I've thought the worst of you. I guess I just..."

He covered her hand with his, ignoring the zip of electricity coursing through him. It was the same current as the last time, which he'd attributed to nerves. Well, that explanation didn't fly this time. "You are *not* a failure. You've fought hard to keep it going. I think you're pretty amazing, in fact."

"I don't feel very amazing." Her response was so soft he nearly didn't hear her.

"Well, you are."

A small smile curved her lips. Man, he liked being

the source of that smile. Most guys liked the flashy smiles, but to Hunter, these were worth more. They were intimate, only meant for one person. For some odd reason, the idea that it was meant for him made him happy.

"So, you said on the plane that we're staying with your brother?" she asked.

He'd half expected her to pull her hand away, and when she didn't, neither did he. Holding hands with her felt right. Then frustration bubbled in him. This was a show, so of course they'd be holding hands. That's what engaged people did, and he needed to get used to it. That was the only reason she was continuing to hold his hand. Practice made perfect.

Nodding, Hunter said, "Yeah, about two years ago, he purchased the ranch that used to be the main draw for Caprock Canyon. He had the home remodeled so we could all stay together during the holidays."

"That was pretty nice of him." She tangled her fingers with Hunter's. "I guess we need to get comfortable holding hands, huh?"

"That's what I was thinking." Which was true, but hearing her say it like that bugged him. They weren't even to the ranch, and he was having problems with this farce. Sunday seemed way too far away already.

"Tell me more about your family. You've been on Tybee Island your entire life, right?"

She nodded. "Never saw any point in leaving. I've loved cooking since I was a kid. For a while, I thought about going to culinary school but decided against it. I've never had any complaints about my cooking."

"I don't doubt that. That chicken whatever was blow-your-mind incredible. It took effort not to reach across the table and steal yours."

Reagan's laugh filled the cab, and he loved it. He glanced at her and could see the little sparkle in her eyes. Another thing about her he liked. The way compliments lit up her face. She grinned wide. "I'm glad you liked it."

"You're going to get along great with Bandit. He's Bear's best friend, but really, the whole family claims him. He's a brilliant cook too. He learned from his mom who owned a restaurant in town. After she passed away, he tried to keep it open, but once the ranch went under eleven years ago, the town slowly died too."

"That's really sad. Why did the ranch shut down?"

"Well, kinda like what happened to you. There were a few years of hard weather. It's expensive running a cattle ranch, and there's a domino effect. Once one thing goes wrong, they begin piling up." He sighed, thinking back to all the times they talked about winning the lottery and what they'd do with the money. "Bear's wanted to buy that ranch forever."

She pulled her hand free. "So, he kinda does what you do."

The regret of mentioning it hit Hunter hard. "No, it wasn't like that."

"You mean rich people deciding they want something and taking it whether the person who owns it agrees or not?"

"No…"

She held her hands up to silence him. "Let's just not talk for a minute, okay?"

His shoulders sagged, but he could see the wall she'd put up. Trying to crack it when she was upset seemed pointless. Maybe by the time they got to the house, she'd be more open to letting him explain that Bear hadn't swooped in and taken the ranch while they were having a hard time. It had sat vacant for ten years. "Okay."

The rest of the drive was spent in silence so tense it felt like fingers pressing against his throat. When he finally turned off the highway onto the stretch of road leading to the ranch house, it seemed like another mile would smother him.

As he parked the truck, he twisted in his seat. "Reagan, this ranch closed down more than a decade ago. The people who used to own it had no money to start it up again. We were kids when it went under, and we weren't rich. My dad lost his job when this place shut down. A lot of people did. We're not bad people." He raked his hand through his hair and sighed. "I'm not a bad guy."

"I know." She turned in her seat to face him and closed a bit of the distance between them by scooting closer. "I'm sorry. I overreacted. I guess I'm just...sensitive."

Yeah, she would be. Not long after he met her, he'd hit her with purchasing her home. *Her home.* Where he saw a business and a nice place to retire, she was seeing memories of her childhood. It had been thoughtless not to even consider that before offering to buy it.

"It's okay. I understand. You have every reason to think poorly of me. I haven't exactly been gentle about wanting your home. And if it were mine, I'd feel the same way." He lifted his gaze to hers. "You may not believe me, but I really do think you're great."

In the next second, her arms circled his neck as she hugged him. "Thank you." She leaned back. "I don't remember there being a time when someone said that about me."

His heart jackhammered in his chest as his gaze dipped to her lips. It was the first time he'd been hit with the temptation to kiss a woman in a long time. "You've been hanging out with the wrong people."

"You think so?"

Before he could answer, someone tapped on the window. They both startled and pulled away from each other.

"Guess it's time to meet the family, huh?" Her cheeks bloomed dark as a red rose.

"Guess so."

Whew. He'd almost kissed her. That would have been a marvelous mess. It was odd putting those two last words together, but it fit. Hunter had no doubt he'd enjoy kissing her, but it would make a mess of things once it was over. As long as they maintained that business line in the sand, they'd both come away unscathed in the romance department.

CHAPTER 8

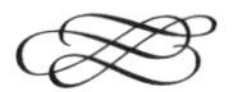

Reagan quickly opened the door of the pickup and jumped out. Thank goodness the man standing in front of her had knocked when he did. She'd been dangerously close to sharing a kiss with Hunter. A complication she didn't need.

Now that she was outside, the chill in the air cleared her head even further. "Wow, it's beautiful here." Wide-open plains, a few horses lining up along the fence, and the bottom of the sun barely touching the horizon. Rusty reds, burnt orange, and purple colored the sky. "Just, wow."

Hunter joined her on the passenger side of the pickup. "Reagan, this is my brother Josiah."

She shook hands with the man. The similarities

were easy to see. Same blue eyes and build. The only difference was height. Josiah was a few inches shorter.

"Hi, Reagan." Josiah smiled and looked at Hunter. "Mom said you were bringing the fiancée. It was about time."

The brothers hugged and clapped each other on the back. "Is everyone here?" Hunter asked.

Josiah nodded. "Yeah, almost. The Fredericks are picking Stephanie up at the airport in Amarillo. They're getting in late. Bear, Dad, and Wyatt found that missing pregnant mare. Bear called and said they'd be awhile. She's having trouble delivering, and they're assisting."

"Assisting?" Reagan asked.

"Life on a ranch. Sometimes we have to step in to help new moms," Hunter replied.

"Oh." She blinked, never having really thought about how a ranch worked or what it was like to take care of large animals. Great Danes were big, but not that big.

Hunter slipped his arm around her waist, and she caught herself before she pulled away. This was the only reason she was in Caprock Canyon. Pretending to be his fiancée. "Is Gabby at the orchard?" he asked.

Josiah nodded. "Yeah, and Carrie Anne and Israel are with her."

"There's an orchard too?" Reagan asked.

"Yeah, Bear found it right before Thanksgiving last year. Our brother Wyatt and his wife, Gabby, purchased it from Bear," Josiah replied. "Maybe mom can take her focus off me and Bear now that you're here."

Laughing, Hunter tightened his hold on Reagan. "That bad?"

She looked up at him. "I think I'm missing something."

"Our mother is desperate for grandchildren."

"Oh." Her eyes widened. Just what had she gotten herself into?

A smile slowly spread on his lips, and he touched them to her forehead. "I'll protect you."

Just minutes ago, she'd caught herself before pulling away, and now, she found herself leaning into him. There was something incredibly intimate about being kissed on the forehead.

Josiah groaned. "Really? In front of me?"

Hunter punched him on the arm. "Shut up. I need to get her settled into her room."

She shivered a little. At first, the brisk air was nice, but it was slowly stealing every ounce of her heat. "Good thing you reminded me to bring that coat."

"Let's get you inside." Hunter pulled away and retrieved their luggage from the back seat.

Just as they shut the front door of the ranch house, an older woman greeted them. "Oh, it's so good to see you," the woman said as she hugged Hunter.

He dropped the luggage and returned the hug. "Glad to be home."

Reagan took a minute to look around at the interior of the home. Warm colors with little splashes of bright hues here and there and stairs to the right leading to the second story. It was about as picturesque as a place could be.

Stepping back, Hunter rested his hand on the small of Reagan's back. "Reagan, this is my mom, Caroline. This is Reagan Loveless, my fiancée."

His mom enveloped Reagan in a hug and squeezed. "It's good to finally meet you."

"Thank you," she said, hugging her back. "I'm glad to meet you too."

His mom grasped Reagan's hands between hers. "You're freezing, sweetheart. Hunter, did you let her come here without a coat?"

Reagan giggled. It was funny seeing him chastised. "No, ma'am, he told me. I just didn't have it on out there."

"Call me Caroline," she said and pointed a finger at Hunter. "She just saved your hide."

He leaned over and pressed a kiss to Reagan's cheek. "Thank you."

Her skin tingled where his lips touched her. Again, a sweet kiss that was every bit as intimate as a regular kiss. Taking a deep breath, she pushed away the notion that either of the kisses meant anything. There was a contract requiring them to act like they were engaged. Kissing just came with the performance.

Straightening, he picked up the luggage again. "I thought I'd show Reagan to her room and then we'd visit more."

"Oh, sure. I'll get us some..." His mom paused. "Reagan, do you like coffee or hot chocolate? Bandit is a whiz with either. Hunter said something about you being a fabulous cook, but you have to be exhausted after traveling."

Reagan jerked her attention to Hunter. "You told her?"

Caroline patted her hand. "Oh, sweetheart, you should have heard him talking about your talent. I swear he was building a pedestal as he spoke."

Tucking a piece of hair behind her ear, Reagan felt her cheeks warm. He'd called her a great cook, but she'd figured it was just him being nice. Not that she didn't know she could cook, but having it recognized made her feel good.

"He's a pretty great guy." The words were out of her mouth so quickly she nearly choked, but it was true. It was sweet of him to talk about her like that.

"Okay, well, you two go find your rooms. I'm guessing you're a hot chocolate fan, right?"

"Yes, ma'—Caroline."

"Count me in for hot chocolate," Hunter said.

"All right, Hunter, get her settled, and we'll see you in a second." His mom smiled.

"Yes, ma'am," he replied and started up the stairs.

They silently ascended the stairs and then stopped when they reached one of the middle bedrooms on the left. He set his luggage down in the hall, and she followed him inside. The bedroom was just as warm and inviting as the living room.

"Uh, is there anywhere special you want me to put this?" Hunter asked, gesturing toward the suitcase.

"No, just leave it by the bed."

He complied, and as he passed her to leave, she placed her hand on his arm. "Your mother seems wonderful. So does Josiah."

A flash of sadness crossed his features. "Yeah, they're pretty great."

"But you don't get to see them often?"

"It's not that. Just...you know how you said you sometimes feel like you can't stack up against your sister?"

She nodded.

"Well, multiply that by four. Bear bought this ranch, Josiah is a top real estate agent in Dallas, Wyatt was a pro bull rider, and my little sister, Carrie Anne, is a teacher. A great teacher. I guess...I guess I just don't feel as successful as them."

This was a side of him she never expected to see. A vulnerability she would have sworn didn't exist just a few weeks ago. She placed her hand on his chest. "The impression I got from your mom was of a very proud parent. I don't think you give yourself enough credit."

A smile quirked on his lips, completing a gaze so smoldering she could hear the whoosh as the air was sucked out of the room. "I guess we're two peas in a pod, huh?"

Her head was screaming, *Move, get away!* while her heart was whispering, *One little kiss wouldn't hurt, right?* In the end, her head won out, and she stepped back. "I guess we should get down there, huh?"

He held her gaze a moment longer. "Yeah, we should. She'll send a search party if we take too much longer."

They stepped into the hallway, and Hunter quickly

stashed his luggage in the room across from hers. As they reached the last few steps, he paused and threaded his fingers through hers. "Here we go."

That's right. This was business. The only thing that happened in that room was a momentary lapse in judgment. He needed a fiancée; she needed funds.

"Yep," she said, adding extra confidence to her words. She wasn't sure who needed to buy it more. Him or her. It was only Wednesday.

Her head had the ball and was ready to do a touchdown dance, and her heart was the referee throwing a penalty. She was in so much trouble.

THE PROMISED HOT chocolate had turned into a smorgasbord of finger foods. Veggie trays, fruits, and little bite-size pastries were brought out. Caroline, Bandit, Hunter, and Reagan were seated around the island in the kitchen. It wasn't until she popped a tomato into her mouth that she realized she was kinda hungry.

Hunter had offered to get something to eat when they landed in Amarillo, but she'd declined. At the time, she was a ball of nerves and the very thought of food made her stomach churn. Now that she thought back, he'd not eaten either.

She leaned over and whispered, "It just dawned on me that you didn't eat earlier."

His breath tickled as he put his lips against her ear. "You said you didn't feel good. I didn't want to get something and make you feel worse."

Color her gobsmacked. None of the men she'd dated in the past had ever been that thoughtful. Not a single one of them. But this man? Every time she turned around, she was seeing a new facet of him. She cupped his jaw and kissed his cheek. "That was kind of you. Thank you."

"So, Reagan, Hunter told us you run a bed and breakfast on Tybee Island. The Sandy Pelican, right?" Caroline asked.

"Yes, it's been in my family for four decades."

"Well, he's had nothing but wonderful things to say about it," his mom said.

"She could show Bandit a thing or two." Hunter laughed. He'd teased Bandit several times.

Reagan bumped him with her shoulder. "Stop that."

"It's true." He smiled.

With a grin, Bandit slid off his stool. "Th-th-that's all right. I d-d-don't mind." At first, Bandit hadn't spoken much, but as time passed, he'd begun speaking more. Reagan suspected he needed to feel comfortable around her.

Caroline leaned forward with her arms on the table. "I am interested in how you two met." She tapped Hunter on the arm. "I can hardly get this one on the phone, and when I do, it's like I'm pulling teeth."

Hunter sat back. "I wanted to buy her bed and breakfast."

Reagan's heart sped up. They weren't going to tell his mom this part. Was he breaking the contract? Before she could interject, a door opened from what sounded like the back of the house, and three men strode into the kitchen.

After they'd cleaned up a little and gave an update about the mare—both the mom and baby were in the barn and doing fine—they introduced themselves as Bear, Wyatt, and King, Hunter's father, and then stood around snacking. It amazed her how close they all seemed. This was a normal gathering for them. If Reagan was honest, she liked it. How much fun would it be to have such a large family and have this every holiday?

"Okay, now that I know the mare is all good, I want to hear the rest of how Hunter met Reagan. He was just telling me as you guys walked in." Caroline looked at Hunter. "Now, finish."

"Well, like I said, I'd stopped in on my way home

one evening because I kept passing her bed and breakfast on the way to work. I'd wanted to buy it, but when she found out, she wasn't very happy with me." He turned his gaze on Reagan and smiled. "She had to be the cutest woman I'd ever seen. The place wasn't doing so well financially, but she has more determination and drive than anyone I've ever met. Not only was she beautiful, but she was someone I respected."

Reagan was nearly gasping for air as he finished. He'd said all that in front of his family, so either he really believed it or he was piling it on high and wide. "I doubt I was that cute or anything else."

"Oh, you were."

The way he was looking at her nearly had her believing he meant every word. But there was no way that was true, right? Even if he did, that didn't mean anything. Maybe he just needed to find a way to sell this whole thing to his family and this is what helped him do that.

Still, she couldn't deny that a part of her liked the idea that he thought of her like that. That he really, truly meant what he said. Oh, her thoughts were spinning so hard she was getting dizzy. One second, she was thinking he was playing a part, and the next, she was wondering if he was being truthful. She needed Sunday to get here and quick.

CHAPTER 9

Hunter slowly shuffled into the kitchen the next morning a little before dawn. It was typical of him. By now, he'd be hurrying out the door and headed to a job site. The smell of coffee beans brewing hit him, and he took a big whiff. Bandit's coffee. The good stuff. Reagan's was probably just as good.

With a little hunting, he found a cup and poured himself some, doctoring it with sugar and cream. He took a sip and looked down at it. This wasn't Bandit's coffee at all. This was a mean trick. How could something smell so good and then taste so awful?

His mom walked into the kitchen and smiled. "Hey, sweetheart. How's the coffee? I went ahead and started a batch."

Horrible, but he had better wits than that. “Uh, it’s good.” He took another small sip and smiled. “Thanks.”

“I told Bandit I’d get up early this year and set the turkey out, but I know him. He’ll probably be in here any second, checking up on me.”

Hunter leaned his hip against the counter and set his cup down. Despite the coffee, he was glad to be home with his family. He’d missed them more than he realized. “Knowing Bandit, that’s probably true.”

She poured herself a cup and took a giant sip. Her lips curled up as she wrinkled her nose and then dumped it in the sink. “You said it was good.”

“I didn’t want to hurt your feelings.” He chuckled.

“Oh, you!” She snatched his cup and set it in the sink. “We’ll wait for Bandit.”

“I’m on board with that.” He hugged his mom. “I’ve missed you, Momma.”

His mom patted his back. “I’ve missed you too, sweetheart.” She leaned back, took his face in her hands, and kissed his cheek. “You’ve been too busy to let us visit. Have you been taking care of yourself over there in Georgia?”

“I guess.”

She sighed and dropped her hands. “Well, at least I know you have someone to make sure you do. I really like Reagan. She is just a cup of joy. And so pretty. Honey, I think you found a keeper."

If only. The instant thought threw him. It was just…a contract. Pretend. But he'd enjoyed spending time with her the day before. Twice, he'd nearly kissed her. Mercy, he'd been more tempted than ever.

Bear joined them in the kitchen, bundled up for work on the ranch. "Nice morning."

Hunter nodded. "Yep, you want some help feeding the animals?"

"I sure ain't stupid enough to turn it down."

"Let me get dressed." Hunter paused at the kitchen entry. "Don't drink the coffee. Momma poisoned it."

Their mom grumbled and threw a dishtowel at him. He dodged and hurried up the stairs. He rushed getting dressed, and moments later, he was downstairs and headed out the door with Bear.

"Are we starting with the cattle?" Hunter asked.

Bear shook his head. "Naw, they've got some good grazing right now."

They reached the barn, and Hunter was blown away. "Wow, Bear, you've really worked on this place."

The once sad-looking barn now sported brand-new paint, but what wowed Hunter was the inside. Not only was it heated, but the stalls were stained in a rich color, and the solid-surface floor sloped so it could be easily cleaned. It gave new meaning to "state of the art." No wonder the horses looked so happy.

"Well, once we got the fencing taken care of, I started working on the fields. While that was going, I got a contractor out here to fix up the barn with all the ideas Wyatt came up with last year around this time. Can't herd cattle without horses or ATVs. And you know Dad..."

"Horses," they said at the same time.

They laughed, and Bear stuffed his hands in his pockets. "Yeah, they don't run out of gas and leave you stranded in the middle of a field."

"True." Hunter drew in a long breath, loving the smell of hay and sweet feed. "You've done an incredible job, Bear. You should be really proud of yourself."

"You could move home and help."

Shaking his head, Hunter said, "I like it in Georgia."

Bear eyed him. "I guess Reagan has something to do with that?"

Before this trip, she hadn't, but spending time with her had already been giving him things to think about. He really liked her. "She's lived there all her life, and I love being near the beach." Two total truths.

"Well, you better have a big enough place for Mom and Dad. When you start having kids, you know she'll be visiting every chance she gets."

Hardly, since the relationship wasn't real. He'd need to find a wife before he even considered having children. Although, children with Reagan didn't sound too bad. "Let's get these animals fed. I need to get back and check on Reagan. I don't need her getting grilled by anyone."

On their way to the feed room, they stopped at the stall that held the mare and her new baby. The momma whinnied as her baby nursed. It sure was a cute little colt with spindly long legs. Bear talked of letting her out to graze, but with it being so chilly that morning, he opted to keep her in until it was warmer.

The chores took longer than Hunter planned, but that's what he got for being gone so long and underestimating the number of animals they needed to feed. After they were all taken care of, they returned to the house. As they stepped through the back door, voices filtered out of the kitchen. One was unmistakably Reagan's. Hopefully, she didn't feel thrown to the wolves.

When they entered the kitchen, Reagan was hunched over a cup of coffee. She wasn't gagging, so most likely Bandit had fixed it.

Hunter crossed the room and stopped next to her. "I'm sorry. I was helping Bear feed the horses."

His mom and Bandit were working together on

Thanksgiving dinner. Hunter wasn't sure what to think of that. He loved his mom, but after that coffee, he wasn't sure he could ever trust her around food again.

"Yep, my fault he wasn't here," Bear replied. He grabbed a cup and poured himself some coffee. "See you folks in a bit. I'm gonna go get washed up." He chugged his drink and left the kitchen.

"Wow, that's a different way to enjoy coffee," Reagan said through a laugh.

"I think he pours it directly into his stomach," Hunter said, slipping onto the stool next to Reagan. "You okay?"

"I'm fine. And good morning to you." She smiled at him. Man, she was some kind of beautiful of a morning: a cute set of pajamas, no makeup, and her hair a little disheveled as it spilled over her shoulders.

"Good morning, beautiful," he said without an ounce of hesitation. He pushed her hair back and pressed a kiss to her forehead. It was as natural and normal as breathing. When he leaned back, her wide eyes were locked with his.

A breath later, she touched his cheek and jerked her hand back. "You're freezing. I'll get you a cup of coffee. Bandit was busy, so I made it."

"You don't have to do that. I can get it."

"Stay," she said as she slipped off the stool. "I can get you some. Cream and sugar, right?"

How did she know that? They'd talked about a lot of things, but he couldn't remember anything about coffee. "Yeah, the sweeter the better."

"You s-s-still drink it that way?" Bandit asked.

"Yes," Hunter answered, and moments later, a steaming cup of coffee was slid in front of him. Wrapping his hands around the mug, he let the warmth thaw his fingers. "Oh, smells good." He took a sip and wilted. "Oh, babe, this *is* good."

"One spoon of sugar." She smiled like she'd won a race.

"Only one?" Boy, it sure didn't taste like it.

"Bandit challenged me. I had to bring my 'A' game." She giggled.

Hunter set the cup down and hugged her to him, kissing her forehead. "That's my girl. You show him how it's done." It wasn't a shock that she fit against him.

Honestly, he'd spent the night thinking about her. He'd liked her the moment he met her. With a little soul-searching, it didn't take long to figure out that purchasing the bed and breakfast wasn't the sole reason he'd been drawn back to the place again and again. It was her.

"Did you sleep okay?" he asked as he leaned back.

She took a deep breath. "Like a log. I guess I needed the break."

He studied her a moment, noting the dark circles had lightened. "Good."

Hunter caught his mom glancing at him and smiling. Well, he was engaged. This is exactly how he'd treat a woman he was in love with.

His sister bounced into the kitchen. "Is this Reagan?" she asked Hunter.

"This is Reagan."

Carrie Anne gathered his fake fiancée in a hug. "I'm Carrie Anne. It's so nice to meet you." She released Reagan and stepped back. "Two brothers down, two to go."

Reagan looked at Hunter, her eyebrows drawn. "What?"

"Wyatt is married, and I'm engaged. Josiah and Bear are on the radar now."

His sister wrinkled her nose. "They just act like they don't want help." She walked to the fridge and pulled out the juice. With a full glass, Carrie Anne again bellied up to the island. "So, have you started picking out dates or dresses?"

Reagan froze.

"We're taking that slow, so no. We haven't yet," Hunter replied.

"I noticed you don't have a ring, Reagan," his mother said, throwing a glance over her shoulder.

Hunter stiffened. A ring. How could he have forgotten the most important part of the act? That should have been the first thing he thought about, but it had completely slipped his mind.

Carrie Anne's mouth dropped. "You asked her to marry you and haven't gotten her a ring yet?"

"Yes, she has a ring," he said. "She was working, and it slipped off. It got caught in the garbage disposal and is at the jeweler being repaired." Talk about thinking fast on his feet. Hunter was proud of that quick response.

His mom stopped chopping sweet potatoes and joined them at the island. "You could let her wear one of Grandma Jo's rings in the meantime. Just until she gets hers back."

Reagan shook her head. "Oh, I couldn't possibly do that."

"Don't be silly. Of course you can," his mother insisted.

Carrie Anne nodded. "I agree."

"Finish your coffee, and then you can take Reagan into Caprock Canyon. Show her the town and go to the house and let her pick a ring." His mom patted Reagan's hand. "And, sweetheart, whichever ring you like, you wear it, okay?"

"How about tomorrow. We just got in yesterday, and honestly, I'm still a little worn from the travel," Hunter said.

His mom sighed heavily. "All right. You have a point." She moved back to the sweet potatoes.

Hunter leaned close to Reagan and whispered, "You don't have to pick out a ring, but I'd be happy to show you the town." His cheek brushed hers, and the touch rattled him. He liked being this close to her.

Her hand came to rest on the side of his face as he pulled back. "I'd love to do that."

Either she was really good or his head was spinning so fast from putting too much thought into it. In the span of a day, he'd gone from wanting her bed and breakfast to wondering what it would be like to have *her*. If they were equally great apart, what would it be like to have both?

He took her hand and kissed her palm. "Maybe we'll dress warm and take a walk while we're there."

Her head bobbed up and down. "Okay."

"Better dress really warm," his dad said as he entered the kitchen. "There's a cold front moving in from the northwest. Weatherman is saying it's going to dip into the forties, and we may even get a couple of feet of snow. It's the Panhandle though, so who knows."

"Couple of feet?" Reagan asked.

"That's the Caprock for you," his mom said. "Add in a little West Texas, and you can have all four seasons in about ten seconds." She laughed.

Hunter put his arm around her waist. "We'll still be able to head back to Tybee by Sunday."

His mom's face fell. "Hunter, I thought you were staying through the holidays like last year."

"Mom, I said I couldn't."

Carrie Anne huffed. "You hardly ever come home. You had to know Mom would want you to stay through the holidays."

"I'll need to discuss it with Reagan first. She has a business to run, and she only planned through Sunday." He looked at her. "We'll talk about it on the way to town."

Reagan nodded. "Sure."

They'd discuss it, but he wasn't going to talk her into staying. She'd already been more than great. His family didn't seem to have any idea it was fake. It wouldn't be fair to ask anything more of her. If he had to take her back to Tybee and then fly back, that's what he'd do.

CHAPTER 10

Thanksgiving with Hunter's family was much like any meal they shared. If she hadn't been told the Fredericks weren't blood-related, Reagan never would have guessed it with how they treated one another. Lots of stories, teasing, and laughter. She caught herself envying their relationships.

At first, it had felt unnatural that she wasn't spending the day cooking. Since she could remember, her holidays were spent working. Then she'd forced herself to relax and enjoy the time off. It had almost been like a day at the spa. Another thing she'd never experienced.

The following morning, a knock came at her door. "Come in," she called out.

Slowly the door opened. "It's Hunter. Just want to make sure you know it's me."

More than once she'd secretly observed him over the past two days, and he was the same person whether she was around or not. It had given her a lot to chew on. Her first impressions of him were turning out to be completely off the mark. He was a wonderful man, kind and thoughtful.

"Come on in," she replied.

A smile greeted her as he walked in wearing pajamas. His hair was sticking up in places, and she could tell he wasn't ready to be up. "I hear you're going Black Friday shopping."

"Yeah, your mom and sister insisted on it." The temperature had dipped lower than the predicted forty degrees, but thankfully, there'd been no snow.

Reagan's parents had never participated in Black Friday. Between not having the funds, and being booked on the weekend, she'd never had the opportunity to go. She was still broke, but she figured being in a group would make it just as much fun as if she had money to spend.

She hoped her change in the day's plans were okay. "So…if you still wanted to, I guess we can tour Caprock Canyon tomorrow since it sounds like shopping will take all day."

"That will work." He seemed a little disappointed. Could he be sad to miss out on a day with her? Wishful thinking.

"Why are you up so early?"

He shrugged. "I…" He crossed the room and sat on the bed next to her. "I'm afraid you'll take this the wrong way."

She knitted her eyebrows together. "What?"

Hunter pulled out a small wad of cash and placed it in her hand. "I know you've been struggling…and…" His shoulders sagged. "I want you to have fun while you're out."

"It's okay. I don't have to buy anything." Plus, taking even more money from him? That wasn't part of the deal.

"But I want you to. I think you deserve to have a little fun."

Reagan looked down at the money, and a plastic card was sticking out. "This is too much."

He shook his head. "I'm a single man who works all the time. Someone should be enjoying it." He lifted his gaze to hers and smiled.

Could he get any kinder? "I feel bad taking this."

"Well, how about we call it…me getting out of going Christmas shopping." He winked. "Plus, they're going to try to talk you into staying through Christmas. You'll probably think it's not enough by the time you get back." He chuckled.

"I really like your family. They're all great."

"I didn't realize how much I missed them until I got here." He took a deep breath and stood. "Anyway, I'll let you finish getting ready."

Setting the money on the bed, Reagan quickly jumped up and touched his arm. "Thank you for…the money to go shopping." Now that she'd said it aloud, she was a little embarrassed.

He tipped her chin up with one finger. "We're a team while we're here. What's mine is yours. Okay?"

A flood of emotion hit her, and she swallowed back tears. A team. How much easier would things be if she were part of a team? Maybe that's how her parents made it seem so effortless.

The longer he held her gaze, the more she wanted him to kiss her. She lifted on her toes and touched her lips to his. "I—"

The sentence was cut short as he took her face in his hands and pressed his lips to hers. It was the gentlest, most wanted kiss she'd ever experienced. One arm wrapped around her waist while his other hand slid up her back and into her hair. She circled her arms around his neck and held on to him.

He coaxed her lips apart, deepening the kiss, and

she was lost in him. It was her and him and whatever this thing was between them. Not enemies, but not exactly friends. One thing she did know with certainty was she liked how it felt being in his arms and being kissed by him.

Just when she thought she'd starve for air, the kiss slowly came to an end with him brushing soft open-mouth kisses along her jaw.

He leaned back and held her gaze once more. She'd never seen a stormier set of eyes, but she was sure he was seeing the same thing in her eyes. What was happening between them?

He swallowed hard, touched his lips to her forehead, and stepped back. "I'll see you later. Have fun, okay?" With that, he turned and left her standing in the room, gawking after him.

Talk about an easy man to fall for. Hunter West was so much more than what she gave him credit for. If she didn't watch herself, she'd be traveling back to Tybee with her heart tied in knots, especially when he kept checking her boxes like he was reading over her shoulder.

REAGAN'S TRIP to Amarillo was spent with Hunter's

mom, sister, sister-in-law, Stephanie, and Mrs. Fredericks chattering endlessly about previous Black Friday adventures. The shock on their faces when Reagan admitted she'd never done it before was funny. After that, they spent the rest of the ride filling Reagan in on their best tips and tricks.

As hard as she tried to listen, her heart and mind were on the kiss she'd shared with Hunter. It had been…beyond incredible. The man she'd thought of as an enemy kissed her with tenderness and want. When was the last she'd been wanted? Long enough that she couldn't remember.

From there, her thoughts drifted to her family and how they might be spending their day. She wished now that they'd done more things like this. Something outside of the bed and breakfast that they could've shared. It wasn't until she noticed the silence that she realized they were all looking at her. That's what she got for momentarily daydreaming.

"I'm sorry. I think I missed something." She smiled.

Carrie Anne smiled as she turned in the seat to face Reagan. "It's okay. I was asking you what it's like to run a bed and breakfast. Hunter said you're a stellar chef."

"Chef is a big word, and I don't have formal training. I've been cooking since I was fourteen, so most of what I know has come from making a lot of mistakes."

"Wow," Carrie Anne replied. "I think I was reading gossip magazines at fourteen and crushing on actors."

Gabby snorted. "Take out the 'I think' part."

Carrie Anne wrinkled her nose at her. "Yeah, well, you were crushing on my brother, so it's not like you were doing anything like cooking either."

Reagan laughed at them. "You two are a riot. I think Naomi and Kaylee would love this."

"Are they your friends back on Tybee?" Carrie Anne asked.

"Yeah, they bicker like the two of you."

Gabby turned in her seat. "I bet it's been hard to stand back and let someone else cook this weekend."

Reagan nodded. "A little." But Hunter hadn't let her do any work. He'd barely let her lift a finger the day before. He'd mentioned the dark circles under her eyes, and he wanted to give her a break because he knew she worked hard. Just another quality she found herself enamored with.

Caroline glanced over her shoulder. "I have to tell you, Reagan. Hunter is smitten with you. He's never brought home a woman before. You saw his love language yesterday—taking care of people. That's why he's so good at flipping houses. He thinks about the people who'll be living there and does things right."

Reagan didn't know what to make of that. He'd never brought a woman home before? And he chose her as his first? He had taken care of her the day before too. Not only that, but on the way to Caprock Canyon, he'd offered to fix her floors. At the time, she was sure it was just him trying to weasel her home out from under her. Now she didn't know what to think.

"I guess he's told you about winning the lottery and being a billionaire. I don't suspect he'd have kept that from you now that you're engaged," Caroline said.

What? Lottery winnings? She had assumed he was rich, but a billionaire? Reagan blinked, working hard not to choke. Good grief and gravy, she'd never bothered to learn how to count that high. What need was there when you knew you'd never be one? Wow. She took a sip of her water and gave herself a second to think.

Clearly, if she was engaged to Hunter, she'd know about the money. That *was* the part she'd signed up for, so she shrugged and said, "Oh, well, he doesn't make a big deal out of it and neither do I." That was certainly the truth.

Carrie Anne nodded. "Honestly, we're the same people before the money. For years, my brothers had played the lottery weekly, never expecting to win. They did it for fun. Believe me, they were floored when the numbers matched."

"They made Carrie Anne claim it with them," Gabby added.

"Yep, they tried to get all of us to do it, but his dad and I weren't going to do that," his mom said.

Mrs. Fredericks nodded. "Us too, but that's our boys." She elbowed Caroline. "We couldn't have better kids."

Reagan chewed the inside of her mouth. What if they thought she was only after Hunter for his money? "Well, we have been looking into a prenuptial agreement."

Carrie Anne's mouth dropped open. "What? That doesn't sound like Hunter. If he loves you enough to marry you, he's planning on forever and whatever it takes to make that happen."

"I just don't want anyone thinking that's why I'm marrying him."

His mom waved her off. "Honey, he'd know if you were, and we trust him. My boy loves you."

Just how skilled was he at lying?

Sheesh. She was pointing a finger at him, and four were leveled right back at her. She was just as guilty for leading them to believe they were engaged. Still, if this was fake love, she had to wonder what being really loved by him would be like.

So far, he'd shown himself to be kind, gentle, and caring. It did sting a little that he hadn't told her about winning the lottery, but could she really blame him? Who knows how many people had tried to use him just for his money. Plus, she'd seen his hands. They were large and calloused like a man who worked for a living. He may have won the lottery, but it didn't win him.

The real question was...did she tell him she knew or feign ignorance? If she told him, it could ruin things if there was a good reason he didn't want her to know. If she didn't and he found out from someone else, would he feel hurt? Reagan knew she would, and the last thing she wanted to do was hurt him. Not after he'd been so wonderful.

She took a deep breath and let it out slowly. Maybe when they toured the town, she'd tell him. They'd be alone. That way, if he was upset, they could figure out a way to deal with it without an audience. By then, the holiday would pretty much be over if he wanted to head back to Tybee.

Inwardly, she wilted. She hated the idea of him leaving early. She could tell he'd missed his family. Hers wouldn't be back until after Christmas. Geez, how did something seemingly simple get so complicated?

Because matters of the heart, no matter how small, were always mountains. Molehills didn't exist in romance.

CHAPTER 11

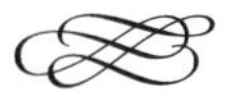

Sunrays stretched like fingers across the horizon as Hunter enjoyed his morning coffee. The kiss from the day before was continually playing in his mind. He'd hoped to talk to Reagan about it, but he'd let her sleep in because she'd returned to the ranch so late after shopping.

On the way out of Amarillo, the Excursion had a flat. What they thought would be a simple fix turned into a two-hour wait. By the time they got home, none of the women were in a mood to do much other than have a bite to eat and go to bed.

Instead of waking her, he practiced some patience and chose to watch the sunrise while he parked himself in a rocking chair on the front porch. Trade the flat desert for a sandy beach and the sound of rushing waves, and he'd be a happy camper. The picture was so clear he could almost smell the salt in the air.

Another thing he could envision was holding Reagan and kissing her again. At first, he'd been a little stunned that she'd planted one on him. Not that he minded. If he were honest, he'd wanted to kiss her, but he'd been a little afraid. It was an answered prayer when she touched her lips to his.

He'd found himself wanting to taste those sweet, soft, kissable lips more and more. They were even better than what he'd imagined. And now they were the only thing he could think about. No, he found himself wanting more. Way more than just a kiss. What he wanted was the two of them cuddled together, watching the sunrise and holding hands as they faced each day's challenges. He'd never thought that way about anyone before.

The front screen door opened, and his mom, bundled in a coat and slippers, stepped onto the porch holding a steaming mug of what he assumed was coffee. "Good morning, sweetheart," she said and kissed his cheek.

"Morning, Mom."

She settled into the chair next to his and held her

coffee cup with both hands. "Nice morning, but a little brisk."

"Yeah, I think that sun out there is teasing us. Those clouds rolling in from the northwest are going to drench us."

She nodded and took a sip of her drink. "I think you're probably right, but we need it. So I'll be grateful for it even if I'm not looking forward to it being cold and wet."

That's how most people in the Panhandle felt about the rain. "Always thankful for the rain. It sure is frosty, though."

"How are you liking it in Georgia?"

He took a drink of his coffee. "I love it. The people are friendly, and the weather is nice. I love the beach."

She glanced at him. "If I ask you something, will you give me a real answer this time?"

He grunted a laugh, suspecting he knew the question she'd ask. "Yeah, Mom, I'll give you a real answer."

"Why did you leave and move so far away?"

Yup, he knew it, but before now, it had been hard to put the answer into words. "I think I needed to prove that I could make something of myself. Wyatt had the rodeo, Josiah is a whiz with real estate, and Bear had worked his way to the top in the cotton ginning business. Carrie Anne's already won Teacher of the Year twice now. Then there's me. I was a nobody in a family of somebodies."

She touched his arm. "Oh, honey. No one thinks that. We've always been proud of you."

Shrugging, he replied, "I wasn't. I needed to get away and figure out who I was and what I wanted. Buying that first house and selling it made me feel independent. I needed time to figure out my place in the world."

"Do you feel like you've done that now?"

"I think so." It struck him as funny. For the first time in his life, he was at peace with who he was and what he'd accomplished. His worth wasn't tied to any one thing; it was tied to the man he wanted to be. Maybe that's why finding a place and putting down roots appealed to him so much.

Silence stretched as Hunter and his mom rocked, watching the sun climb inch by inch.

His mom finished her coffee and cleared her throat. "Do you think you'll ever move back?"

He shook his head. "I really love Tybee Island. To me, it feels like home. I think that's where I want to hang my hat." He looked at his mom. "I'm sorry."

"If that's where you want to be and you're happy there, that's fine with me. Just make sure you get a place on the beach with plenty of bedrooms." She smiled.

With a nod, he chuckled. "Yeah, that was my plan."

"So Reagan..." His mom side-eyed him.

His pulse jumped. "Reagan what?"

His mom stood and smiled. "I really like her. She's sweet, and her coffee is delicious. Plus, she agreed with me that you don't get home often enough, so she said she'd love to stay until New Year's."

"Mom, she has a bed and breakfast to run." And if she'd agreed to stay, it probably meant she also had zero reservations.

His mom nodded. "I know, and I made sure she knew she didn't have to change her plans for me."

"Well, then I guess we'll stay."

She patted him on the shoulder on the way to the door. "When she wakes up, take her into town and let her pick a ring."

"Yes, ma'am."

"Hunter?"

The question in her voice caused him to twist in his chair to look at her.

"You are a sweet man. Reagan is a sweet woman. I think the two of you make a good pair. Dad agrees with me." She winked and left him on the porch alone.

Hunter relaxed back in his seat and slid down,

setting his ankle over his knee. Whew, for a second, he wondered if his mom knew his relationship was fake. That would have been a hard thing to explain.

His mom was right, though. Reagan was sweet, she could cook, and her coffee was out of this world. For a simple guy like himself, those were three of the top qualities he'd want in a partner. Lucky for him, it would take a page to list all the wonderful things about her.

Maybe if Reagan had really agreed to stay through New Year's, they could explore that partnership. He'd sure like to. Hopefully, she'd be open to it.

AFTER FINISHING HIS COFFEE, Hunter had helped Bear with the animals again. When they returned to the house, Hunter paused as he heard Reagan's laughter coming from the kitchen. Not just hers, but Bandits. It reminded Hunter of the prior year when Gabby had pretended to date Bandit.

At the time, Hunter hadn't understood what the big deal was, but he now had a new appreciation for Wyatt's feelings. As he listened to Bandit and Reagan talking and laughing, he could feel his chest tightening. Jealousy was rearing its ugly head at how well they seemed to be getting along.

Shrugging off his coat, he shook off the feeling. Bandit was a good guy, and Reagan was a guest. Aside from that, Bandit was more like a brother than a friend, and he wouldn't go after a woman he knew was taken.

Once his coat was hung up, he slowly walked into the kitchen. Bandit and Reagan had their backs to him, and it was as he expected: two chefs speaking each other's language. They'd cooked a feast, and it warmed him to see her as part of his family. Hunter had no trouble seeing a future with her.

Once the family was together, they took the prepared dishes to the dining room so they could eat breakfast together. The jealousy he'd felt earlier came back stronger as he watched Bandit and his...title-to-be-determined girl laugh and kid while they all sat around the dining room table eating. Hunter knew it was innocent, but his heart and insides were in a turmoil.

What if Carrie Anne had put Bandit up to pretending to be interested in Reagan to make Hunter jealous? He pushed the thought away as he realized how ridiculous it sounded. It wasn't like Wyatt and

Gabby. Hunter and Reagan were engaged. There'd be no reason to pull a stunt like that.

Somehow, he kept that from showing while everyone ate. Once the meal was over, Bandit and Reagan were told to go away so the rest of the family could get the dishes cleaned.

Now, he was standing at her door, debating whether he should talk to her or not. He lifted his hand to knock, and the door swung open. Reagan bounced off him, and he grabbed her before she could fall. "Whoa."

A tiny squeak popped out, and she looked up at him. "I'm so sorry."

"Where are you going in such a hurry?"

"Bandit was going to share some recipes with me, and in turn, I was going to show him how I make coffee." She smiled.

"Oh, okay. I guess I'll talk to you later, then," he said softly, dropping his hands from her arms and turning to walk away. Maybe he had read her intentions with Bandit wrong after all.

She buried her hand in his shirt, bringing him back to face her. "It's just recipes. They won't take long. Now, why were you at my door?"

"Well, I was going to make sure you were okay

staying through New Year's. I know my mom can work the guilt like a pro." He laughed.

She lowered her gaze. "It's okay. I didn't have any reservations anyway, unfortunately, even though holidays are supposed to be a peak time for tourism. I don't mind staying."

He hadn't meant to remind her of the sad state of her business. "I was…I was also going to see if you wanted to go into town with me, but if you're busy, it's okay." That was what his lips were saying, but his heart was screaming, *It's not okay at all!* He tried to keep the disappointment out of his voice.

"Actually, I'd like that. I'd love to see your childhood home and take a walk." She lifted on her toes and kissed him. "I like Bandit, and I love cinnamon rolls. But, I like you more than either one of them."

"Would you mind making it a date?" He smiled as relief filled him. He'd known there was nothing going on, but hearing it certainly helped.

Her eyes twinkled, and she nodded. "I'd really like that. What should I wear?"

Slipping his arm around her waist, he pulled her close. "You can wear anything you want. I think you're beautiful in anything." He cupped her cheek and lowered his lips to hers. Just as sweet and soft as last time. He pulled back and locked eyes with her. "Do you have a dress to wear?"

"Yeah," she whispered. "I have a dress."

"Okay. I can't imagine you prettier than you already are, but so far, you've managed to change my mind every time I see you." He kissed the tip of her nose. "I'll see you in a bit, okay?"

"Uh-huh."

He touched his lips to hers once more and strode to his room, determined to show her a great time. That is, after a cold shower or ten. Twice now, she'd kissed him, and both times the earth had moved under his feet.

When he thought of the future, he could see an outline with two people holding hands, walking the beach at sunset. The longer he was in her presence, the more in focus those two people became. By the time the holidays were over, he wasn't sure he'd want the bed and breakfast anymore. At least, not if it didn't come with her. It wouldn't be worth having.

Bracing his hand against the wall in his bedroom, he closed his eyes and took a deep breath. He needed to slow down. Savor the moment and keep things at a steady pace. For both their sakes.

There was also the issue of the contract. What if she was just playing a part? If he ran full steam ahead and it turned out that she wasn't feeling the same as him, there was a good chance his heart would be crushed.

He'd been lonely a long time, and now that a spotlight was trained on it, he realized the depth of it. What if an act was all this was? Could he be reading too much into their interactions? She had kissed him. Twice. It was circular reasoning at its best and enough to make his head hurt.

With a groan, he pushed off the wall and kicked off his boots. Lonely. Yeah, that was true, but Reagan more than filled that spot. Still, it was better to walk than run. Otherwise, he could face-plant, and he didn't want that outcome for either of them.

CHAPTER 12

During the drive to town, Reagan had debated over and over how she'd tell Hunter she knew about the lottery. The longer she kept it from him, the worse she felt. What if he found out she knew from someone else? When she thought back to their financial interactions, she worried that the times she'd asked for more money or had taken money he'd offered would be looked at differently, like she was gold-digging. Surely he would believe that she didn't know. Would he hate her or question her growing affection for him?

The thought made her heart race. Growing affection? Well, she couldn't deny it. Hunter was a sweet man and someone she enjoyed being with. His kisses were mind-melting, especially that last kiss. It was something straight out of a fantasy. He'd pulled her flush against him, kissed her, and then told her she was beautiful. Plus, the little kiss on the nose? Holy wow. It had been such a little thing but so, so intimate.

"Uh, Reagan?" The sound of Hunter's voice broke through her thoughts.

She smiled. "I'm sorry." Now she realized the truck was parked and the engine was silent. How long had they been sitting in front of his childhood home? "I…"

What if she told him and he *did* get angry? Could she really risk losing the other half of the money? It wasn't her fault that she'd found out, but they'd started this trip as barely friends. What if he didn't believe her?

"Are you okay?"

For now, she'd act as if she had no idea. "Yeah, I'm fine."

He took her hand and smiled. "Come on. Let me show you the house. After we get your ring, we'll take a walk around town before dinner."

For a man who thought he lacked charm, he sure had a lot. "Okay."

He helped her out of his side of the truck, and what she found herself liking more than anything was that he kept holding her hand when he didn't have to.

The outside of his parents' home appeared to be

freshly painted, and the wrap-around porch looked perfect for an early morning swing and watching the sunrise. She could imagine Caroline and King rocking back and forth. "This is a cute house."

"I think so."

They walked to the door, continuing to hold hands. He opened it and held it for her to enter first.

Her mouth dropped open as she stepped inside. "It wasn't locked?"

"There's no one in this town who'd steal. I don't know that we've ever locked a door. Everyone knows everyone," he said, following her in.

Reagan looked around the modest living room. Compared to the home at the ranch, this one was tiny, but it had been updated recently. "I love the colors. The soft gray is nice."

"Yeah, we all pitched in and had the house remodeled earlier this year. I would have done it myself, but I was in the middle of a few projects at the time." He let go of her hand and turned in place. "The men who worked on this did a really good job."

She studied him as his gaze roamed over the room. Somehow, he'd grown more attractive since they'd arrived in Caprock Canyon. He was gorgeous from the get-go, but now...now it went so far beyond looks. She'd peeked into his heart and found gold. "You really enjoy remodeling homes, don't you?"

He brought his attention back to her and nodded. "I do. Or better, I did."

"Did?"

"Guess if anyone's going to know first, it should be you. I finished my last house before we left Georgia. When I return, I'm going to ask Stone, my partner, if he wants to buy my share of the business." He inhaled long and slow like he felt the words now that they were out.

Reagan approached and leaned in to catch his gaze. "You seem sad about that."

A tiny smile lifted his lips. "Not sad. Just…torn. In a way, I feel like I'm leaving my success behind. I've flipped houses so long now that it feels like I'm having one of my legs kicked out from under me. I mean, I know that's not true, but change isn't easy."

She touched her fingers to his temple then slid them down the side of his face and along his jaw. His eyes closed as he pressed his face into her hand. They stood there, letting the silence encase them and shut the world out.

"It's not true. You can't leave success behind, Hunter. It's who you are. The rumor on Tybee Island was that this house flipper wasn't like all the others.

He used quality material, paid close attention to details, and worked efficiently so he could offer solid, well-built homes that lasted. Every home you've touched is a standing reminder to your success."

His eyes opened, and their gazes locked. "You think so?"

Before spending time with him? No. But now? "With all my heart."

"You don't think I'm a bad guy anymore?"

"Let's not get hasty." She chuckled, making sure he knew she was teasing.

He flashed her lopsided grin. "You're not that funny."

It only made her laugh harder.

"Come on, comedian, let me show you the rest of the house." He placed the flat of his hand on the small of her back, and that electric connection climbed her spine, frying her nerves the entire way up.

Each room had a story, and with each story, she learned more and more about him. When they reached his room, she looked it over, seeing little bits and pieces of him all over it.

"How long has it been since you stayed here?" she asked, turning to face him.

Hunter put his hands on his hips and blew out a puff of air. "Uh, maybe two or three Christmases ago."

"I can't picture all of you crowded into a house this small, but I bet you didn't notice it too much, huh?"

"No, but now that Bear has that ranch house, there's no denying it's nice to have a little extra room. I can't tell you how many times I had a drink spilled on me." He laughed.

She nodded. "I can see that being a problem."

He took a deep breath and tipped his head toward his mom's bedroom. "Let's find you a ring out of Grandma Jo's jewelry box."

"Okay."

He led her back to his mom's room, pulled the jewelry box from the shelf in the closet, and sat on the bed. She joined him on the bed as he opened the lid and a tiny ballerina sprang up. "There is all sorts of stuff in here. We call it Grandma Jo's, but it's more like generations of women in my family."

Reagan moved things around, marveling at all the little rings, earrings, and necklaces filling the box. Some looked older than she was comfortable wearing, especially since their engagement was fake. The last word caused her to pause. "I don't know if I can wear any of these. Our…engagement isn't real. I don't want something to happen or to lose it."

"I trust you. Besides, I'm more scared of my mom than you losing that ring."

She leveled her eyes at him. "Then you pick it."

"Okay."

After a few minutes of digging, he pulled out a ring with an aquamarine center lined with little diamonds. She was intrigued that he'd picked it. "What made you pick that one?"

He lifted her left hand, and as he slipped the ring on her finger, he said, "It's bright and soft at the same time. Soothing and peaceful like the ocean." He lifted his gaze to hers. "Like you."

Her heart had climbed higher into her throat with each word spoken. It was sweet and sincere and wonderful, just like him. How had she not seen it before? Warmth spread from her chest to her face and raced to the tips of her ears. No one had ever said anything like that to her before. She was speechless. "I don't know what to say to that."

With a smile, he brought the back of her hand to his lips and pressed a kiss to it. Every nerve in her body felt frazzled and frayed. "How about don't. Let's go take that walk."

Walk, run, jog, jet-fuel backpack, maybe even parachuting out of a plane...wherever he went, she'd be up for it. Okay, the plane thing not so much, but she'd be there for moral support if that's what he liked doing for fun.

Inwardly, she groaned. She needed to tell him she knew about his money, but how? It wasn't fair that he was being so great. This trip was supposed to end with her on one side and him on the other. Instead, the idea of not having him next to her made her want to cry. Maybe she'd figure out a way to tell him before the evening was over because she wasn't sure she could keep it from him much longer.

CHAPTER 13

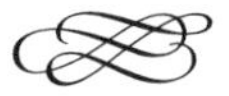

"So, what do you think of Caprock Canyon?" asked Hunter.

Their date so far had been fantastic. When he'd picked the ring out, he'd been afraid he'd said too much, but when he lifted his gaze to hers, the smile on her lips and the twinkle in her eyes were enough to melt him. He couldn't understand why she hadn't been told those kinds of things more often.

Reagan looked at him. "I love it."

He pointed to the building where Gabby worked. "When Gabby isn't at the orchard, she's there. The newspaper shut down not long after the ranch, and when she returned home, she got it going again."

"Neat. Do you think the town will come back now that the ranch is working again?"

He put his arm across her shoulders, bringing her closer. "We hope so. There aren't many of us here, but it's a great place to live and raise a family. Not really much to look at in terms of scenery, but the sunrises and sunsets can't be beat."

"I still can't get over not locking the doors."

"One of the perks of a tiny town." He chuckled. "I'm getting cold and hungry. Are you?"

She nodded. "I think I'm walking on icicles. My legs are freezing."

He groaned. "I should have thought about that when I asked you to wear the dress."

"I think I would have worn it anyway." She smiled.

"Well, you look incredible, but that wasn't a surprise." He knew this thing had started as a business proposal, but the longer they were together, the less business it felt.

She bumped him with her shoulder. "You don't look too bad yourself."

He pulled her to a stop and puts his arms around her. "Is that so," he teased.

Her eyes dipped to his lips and back up, catching his gaze, and in an instant, he couldn't breathe. If sultry had a picture next to it, it would be Reagan Loveless. Mercy, she did things to him that no woman had ever done. Lifting on her toes, she ran her hands from the collar of his coat down the lapel and buried her fists in it. "You were lying when you said you had no charm, Mr. West." Her breath mingled with his, and his mouth went dry.

Swallowing hard, he said, "Uh." Twenty-six letters in the alphabet, and all he had was *uh?*

"Cat got your tongue?" *She* was a cat playing with a mouse.

"Uh. No?" His vocabulary needed serious work.

She chuckled and pulled him closer. "Was that a statement or a question?"

This time she didn't let him answer. She pulled his lips down to hers, wrapping her arms around his neck.

He was flat-out undone. She teased his lips open, and the hunger he felt for her was soul deep. Not just for her kisses, but for every ounce of her, including her imperfections.

He slid his hand up her back, into her hair, and felt the low moan in her throat. Knowing he was the cause only fueled the need for her. When she broke the kiss, she seemed as breathless as he was. He touched his forehead to hers and continued to hold her.

"I've never kissed anyone like that before," she said, her ragged breath matching his own.

"I've never been kissed like that before." A few thousand more wouldn't hurt either.

"That's a very good response." She chuckled.

He pressed his lips to her forehead and brushed them down the side of her face. "I think we should probably go have dinner now."

"I think you might be right." She tilted her head, allowing him easier access, and he continued pressing light kisses along her jaw and across her neck. Another soft moan escaped her lips. "We can go in a minute."

With that, her fingers tangled in his hair as he brought his lips back to hers. He had no idea how long they stood in the middle of the town kissing, but when they broke apart again, the sun was definitely lower in the sky and the temperature had dropped.

She laid her head against his chest, clinging to him. "We can go now."

"Okay." So not okay. He could have spent eternity kissing her and being kissed by her.

Straightening, she held his gaze a second. "I'm kinda glad you wanted to steal my bed and breakfast now." A smile slowly spread on her lips, and all he could do was laugh.

They threaded their fingers together as they walked back to his pickup. When they reached it, he held the door as she got in. The drive to Amarillo was quicker than it had ever been. Mostly because he enjoyed being with her so much. It always felt like there wasn't enough time.

Once they arrived at the restaurant, they were seated at a table near the back. Hunter hadn't tried the place before, but when he'd looked it up online, it had great reviews. Based on what he was seeing and smelling, they were right.

"I don't know if it is their cooking, but I think I could eat a trough full," Reagan said, leaning in. Before he could take the seat across from her, she'd taken his hand, pulling him into the booth next to her. "I'm with you." His stomach grumbled, putting an exclamation on the statement.

Chuckling, she nodded, and then her stomach did the same thing. That made her laugh a little harder. "I guess we were both hungry."

"Seems so."

A waitress stopped at their table, and they ordered their drinks and a fried pickle appetizer.

Once the waitress was gone, Hunter angled himself toward her. "I'm bothered that you don't have reservations for Christmas. I know you may not believe it, but I do want you to be successful."

Her shoulders sagged. "Yeah, I didn't realize how

tight things were for my mom and dad. I thought I could come in and make a few changes and that would fix it. Nothing I tried worked. Then the hurricane tore through the island. It was one thing after another."

Hunter understood that better than she knew. "That sounds like my first flip. It turned out okay, but it was discouraging for the first few weeks. We went from needing a few upgrades to needing new electrical lines run. The roof had warped boards, so that increased the cost. Then, we were robbed, and our tools were taken. At that point, I was ready to give up."

"I can't see you ever wanting to give up."

The tips of his ears warmed from the compliment. At least, that's how he took it. "I did. That first year was so hard. I was on my own for the first time. I felt like I was competing against my siblings."

She nodded. "I know that feeling too. My sister always does things perfectly. I'm the oldest, you'd think I'd have my ducks in a row, but I've come to realize I don't have ducks. I have squirrels with issues."

Hunter belly laughed. "I'm sorry. That's not funny. I promise."

Reagan pouted. "Laughing at me."

The waitress returned to the table with their drinks and offered to give them more time to look over the menu.

When the waitress was out of earshot, Hunter scooted closer, wrapped a lock of Reagan's hair around his finger, and smiled. "I'm not laughing at you. When I look at you, I see a woman I respect and admire."

"Really? Because I always feel like a failure."

"Failure is giving up. You *are not* a failure."

She lowered her gaze and slowly nodded. "I just wish I didn't feel that way all the time. I love my family, but just once I wanted to hear that I'd done something right. I could cook the entire night, have people fawning over my dishes, and all they could hear was the one person who felt their chicken was too dry."

His parents had never done that. Not even the Fredericks had done that. To have lived with that pressure and still have such drive to succeed was impressive. "I can't imagine living under that scrutiny. No one is perfect, and dwelling on what isn't doesn't inspire perfection." He tipped her chin up with his finger. "Reagan, I know my opinion might not carry much weight, but you are talented, kind, and warm. You are perfectly imperfect. I like you just as you are."

Her bottom lip trembled. "That's nice of you say."

"It's what I consider a nice fact." He smiled and touched his lips to hers.

When he pulled back, her eyes locked with his, and even in the dim lighting, he could see she was struggling with what he'd said. His hope was that he'd get the chance to show her how wrong her parents were.

Before she could say anything, the waitress returned with their appetizer. By the time their meals arrived, the sadness he'd felt pouring off her had eased, and she laughed a little more.

Earlier in the day, he'd booked a last-minute adventure for her. His hope was that it would cheer her up so their night could end on a positive note. He hated that she'd been hurt by the very people who were supposed to build her up.

Once they'd finished dinner and were outside, he turned to her. "Close your eyes, okay?"

"Why?"

"Trust me."

A pained expression crossed her features as her lips turned down. She palmed his chest and sighed. "I've been trying to figure out all night long how to tell you something. I just...I just didn't know how to tell you without you getting upset."

His eyebrows knitted together. "Tell me what?"

"On the trip to Amarillo for Black Friday, they were all talking, and then your mom turned to me and said that you'd won the lottery." She stepped into him.

"I didn't know what to do or what to say. I'm supposed to be pretending to be your fiancée, and she said that since I was, she knew you would have told me."

Hunter stepped back, his ears buzzing as his heart dropped to his shoes. Why would his mom even bring up the lottery? It wasn't something they really talked about anymore. At first, yeah, that's all they'd talked about because it was suck a shock, but anymore? It was a non-subject. He worked hard to keep his money a secret.

"Hunter, I promise I had no idea. I felt trapped and acted like I already knew. I've been agonizing over it all night. Knowing doesn't change anything for me, and I'm sure you kept it to yourself for some reason. When you asked if I trusted you, I just couldn't keep it in any longer. Because I do trust you."

As he tried to process what she'd just said, the horse-drawn carriage arrived.

"This was the surprise?" she asked.

"Yeah."

"I'm so sorry I didn't tell you sooner. I—"

He held up his hand to silence her. "Give me time to think, okay?"

Reagan lowered her gaze. "Okay. We don't have to go on the carriage ride. I understand."

"No, I planned this for you. It's already here, and this is a great way to see the lights around the city."

"Okay."

Hunter helped her into the buggy and sat beside her. After they covered their legs with a blanket, the ride started. He put his arm around her, and she snuggled against him.

All night long, he'd been looking forward to this exact moment: her nestled next to him with his arm around her. Now, he didn't know how he felt or what he wanted. Had his mom told her, or did Reagan look it up when they first met?

When she'd asked for a full year's worth of payments, he'd wondered then, but he'd asked her about it. Her reason felt legitimate at the time. Only now that he was thinking back, he was tired, stressed, and desperate. Had his desire to keep his mom from being disappointed clouded his judgment?

Why would his mom even think to bring it up? Could Reagan have said she only wanted the payments instead of the pay-off just to lull Hunter into letting his guard down?

At the moment, he didn't know what to believe. Maybe he needed to take a step back and reevaluate the entire situation. He'd jumped in way too fast with wanting a relationship.

Closing his eyes, he pushed the thoughts to the side and tried to enjoy the moment. He'd figure out what he needed to do when he'd slept on it.

CHAPTER 14

All through the carriage ride, as much as Reagan wanted to believe things were okay, they weren't. They'd gone from passionate kisses worthy of Oscars to barely speaking in the span of a few minutes. Every second, the chasm grew larger, and she had no idea how to stop it.

He'd been so sweet...*perfectly imperfect*. It had been a good thing she was sitting down when he'd used that phrase. If not, she'd have swooned right there in the restaurant. It was without a doubt the most wonderful thing anyone had ever said to her.

Then he'd asked her to trust him, and it had felt like she had no choice but to tell him she knew about the money. The second the words were spoken, she'd seen and felt the shift. He'd retreated so quickly he was a blur.

Once they finished the tour, it was another two hours of silence. She tried over and over to talk about something…anything, but the wall he slammed between them was thick, tall, and impenetrable.

He cut the truck's engine and sat there a moment, inhaling long and slow. "I'm going to need some time to sort this out. I know we have to keep up pretenses for my parents. Because as much as I don't want them to know I'm actually single, I'm even less inclined to tell them the nature of our relationship."

"Okay," she said softly. How was she supposed to get through until New Year's if it was going to be like this? "If you want, I can tell them Naomi and Kaylee have had things come up and I need to go home. If it'll make it easier on you."

He shook his head. "I'm already lying, and I'd like it if I didn't have to add another one to it. Like I said, give me some time to digest this, okay? I'm not mad. I'm just…well, to be honest, I'm not sure what I am at the moment."

Reagan nodded. "I understand. I'll stay out of your way until you're ready to talk to me. When you are, you know where I'm staying." She opened her door, quickly jumped out, and didn't look back.

She really had no reason to lie to him. And that his mother told her? What would be the point in lying about that? He could just ask to verify with his mom. But she couldn't be too upset about it. Money changed things. The more you had, the harder it was to trust someone.

As she reached her room, her phone in her clutch rang. She pulled it out. Her eyebrows knitted together as she looked at the caller ID. Why was Naomi calling her so late? Then again, who knew with her. She wasn't a wild child, but she did get herself in predicaments at times. Which made Reagan even more curious about her call.

"Hey, Naomi, what's going on?"

"Reagan, have you been following the weather?"

She'd checked it before she left for Thanksgiving, and there was nothing on the radar. "I did before I left, why?"

Naomi hesitated a second. "A hurricane is headed toward the island. It's supposed to be here tomorrow night. We've boarded up the house the best we can, but it's going to be a king tide. They're saying it's going to be worse than Irma. They've ordered an evacuation of the island."

If Reagan were hollowed out with a trowel, there would have been more left of her than there was currently. Tears clouded her vision as she sank to the floor in her doorway. "The house?"

"I'm sorry, Reagan," Naomi said. "I would have called sooner, but earlier today they said it was turning. Now it's not, and they're saying with the way it's moving, it's going to be a direct hit."

Before replying, Reagan steadied her voice. "You know what, I'm sure it'll be okay. We've gotten through worse. You and Kaylee stay safe, okay?"

"I know you, Reagan. You can try that tough-girl thing on someone else."

Reagan swallowed hard. "I'm in Texas, and there's nothing I can do. It's not a tough-girl thing; it's facing reality."

For a moment, the line stayed silent. "We love you. You're not alone in this."

But she was. It was her bed and breakfast, and she had no idea how she was going to rebuild again. As tired as she was already, she wasn't sure she even had it in her to start again. "Let me go. I'm going to watch the weather for a while. Maybe it'll turn again. There's always that chance." In her gut, she knew things were going to be bad. It seemed the world had been out to get her since she'd taken ownership of The Sandy Pelican. Why would it have a change of heart now?

"Okay, just remember we love you, okay?"

"Love you too."

The second Reagan ended the call, she put her hand to her mouth, trying to hold in the gut-deep sob. Another hurricane. Another one. She remembered Irma. It was awful, but her parents had rebuilt. How was she supposed to do that? She'd just gotten current on the mortgage. There was the year's worth of payments and the little extra, but not enough to completely rebuild.

She braced her forehead against the doorframe and pressed her other hand to her mouth. It was late, and even if she did wake someone up, there was nothing they could do. By now, she wouldn't even be able to get to the house if she left that minute. She was ruined.

All the height marks, the little wall drawings carefully hidden by furniture, and the creaky step that ratted on her and her sister when they tried to sneak out. All of it was going to be gone. With every memory, more silent sobs tore through her.

"Reagan?" Hunter said.

The last thing she wanted was him seeing her like this. His comfort wouldn't even be real right now. It would only be because he felt sorry for her, and she didn't want anyone's pity. She tried to stand and failed.

"Reagan, I'm sorry. Just give me some time to think."

Lifting her gaze to his, she said, "It's not about you."

His eyebrows knitted together. "Then what?"

Her lips trembled and more tears fell. Her dam was broken. "Hurricane. King tide. It'll be gone. All gone. All that work for nothing. I know it's part of living on the island, but I tried so hard. I worked hard." She lifted her gaze to his. "I didn't ask for anything from anyone. Why me?"

"Oh, Reagan, I'm sorry." In seconds, Hunter kneeled next to her, pulling her to him and holding her. "It's okay. It's going to be okay."

A couple of doors opened, and his mom, his dad, and Josiah came into the hall. Next thing she knew, she was surrounded by the entire clan, all of them witnessing her complete meltdown, but at the moment, she couldn't think. What was she going to do?

"Hunter, what happened?" his mom asked.

"A hurricane's going to hit the island. It's bad."

His mom rushed over and placed her hand on Reagan's shoulder. "Oh, honey, I'm so sorry."

Now that more people were offering comfort, she was crying even harder. What kind of broken toy was she? They were being nice, and she was ugly crying like it was her job.

"Is there anything we can do," Josiah asked. "Anything?"

Reagan shook her head and worked to calm herself. "No," she said with a hiccup. "It's a hurricane. The only thing you can do is try to get far enough inland that you're safe. Tomorrow is a full moon, so in addition to the surge from the storm, there will be the tide too. It's called a king tide, and it's just life on an island."

She squeezed Hunter's bicep. "You need to call Stone and see if he's okay."

"I will, but I'm pretty sure he's already handled it," Hunter replied. He rocked back on his heels, stood, and then helped her up. "I'll see if I can find anything out from him about the storm. Maybe he'll know something. I'll have him check the bed and breakfast."

Exactly what she didn't want. Hunter wouldn't even be speaking to her if it weren't for that stupid hurricane.

His mom pulled her into a hug. "It's gonna be okay, sweetheart. You're one of us now, and we make a great team."

Inside, she wilted. Why did his mom have to say that? Reagan didn't have a team because all of it was pretend. A ridiculous hoax, all to save her home and business, and now, it was all for nothing. Why was she even staying with the Wests at this point? It wasn't like the rest of the money would even come close to helping her keep it. But she wouldn't back out of the deal just because it was now pointless.

Besides, even if she did tell them the truth, she couldn't return to Tybee. With a mandatory evacuation order, they wouldn't allow her access for days or even weeks. She was helpless…and worn out.

Taking a deep breath, Reagan forced herself to get it together. "I appreciate that, Caroline. If you all don't mind, I'm going to go lie down and try to get some sleep."

"Are you sure?" his mom asked.

Forcing a smile, Reagan nodded. "Yeah, I'm sure. Thank you for checking on me."

Caroline took her hand and patted it. "Sure, sweetheart. If you need anything, just let us know, okay?"

"Okay." Reagan held the smile in place until she stepped into her room. She wasn't okay. She was tired, hurt, and sad. Hopeless and helpless. Which seemed to be a way of life for her. If Carlin had taken over the bed and breakfast, it would probably be doing great.

"I know you're not okay." Hunter's voice was soft. It almost made her think things were fine, but they weren't. She was already pretending to be his fiancée, and that was all she had in her at the moment.

She crossed the room to her bed, set her clutch on the nightstand, and raked her hand through her hair. Tears threatened to spill again, but she forced them back. "I've been on my own a long time, Hunter, and while I appreciate the kindness, I can only pretend so much. Could you just leave me alone for a while?"

Heartbeat after heartbeat, he was silent until she heard him take the doorknob. "I'm here if you need anything, okay?"

Reagan nodded. "Yeah." As soon as the door was shut, she crawled onto the bed and curled into a ball.

Whatever spirit she'd had left shriveled up and died. For the first time since she'd taken over The Sandy Pelican, she felt defeated. Not just that, flattened. She was holding on to something with both hands, and everything was doing its best to pry her hands off. How much more did she have to give before something good happened?

It seemed her fate in life was to be on the precipice of something great, only to see it slip from her fingers. Nothing ever seemed to work in her favor. Not with Hunter. Not with the bed and breakfast. Not with anything. For the first time in her life, not a single inch of her had an ounce of hope left.

CHAPTER 15

Once again, Hunter found himself at Reagan's door, hesitating to knock on it. The past week, the tension between them was like an extra person in the room. He was still struggling with her knowing about his money, and she was stressed about her business, especially since they still weren't letting people back on the island yet. It was a combination guaranteed to cause issues.

The hurricane had hit the island, but it had shifted farther south than predicted. It was good news, and at first, Reagan seemed to have handled it well. The last couple of days, though, she'd become withdrawn, and he was worried about her at this point. Not to mention, he was tired of his mom asking him about it. The last straw was Reagan missing lunch.

Frustrated with himself, he knocked on her door, hoping he could talk to her. When she didn't answer, he knocked again. "Reagan, can we talk please?"

When she didn't answer, he knocked again. "Reagan." No answer. He turned the knob and cracked the door a bit. "I'm coming in, so if you're not dressed, it's your fault because I'm warning you."

Silence.

He groaned and pushed the rest of the way in, finding her cross-legged in the middle of the bed with papers strewn all around her and headphones on. "At least you weren't ignoring me on purpose."

With that, she looked up and pulled off her headphones. "You could have knocked."

"I did. You didn't answer."

She lifted an eyebrow. "Perhaps I didn't answer because I didn't want to talk to you."

He grumbled under his breath. "Well, *I* want to talk to you." His attention drifted to the mess of papers spread out around her. "What are all these papers?"

She shrugged. "I wasn't sure what we were going to be doing here, so I brought the financial records for the bed and breakfast. I'm certain the roof is history. I can't do it myself, so I'll have to contract that out. Same with the floors because they'll have damage as well. But the rooms, I think I can do that.

I've watched a few videos on it, and it doesn't seem that difficult. Most of the cost for that will be materials."

"I've been worried about you. I thought..." He crossed the room and sat on the edge of the bed. "I thought you'd..."

"Given up? I want to. It seems I'm fighting an uphill battle. With the storm damage, it'll take a while before tourism bounces back. In the meantime, I've still got the equity line to pay." She sighed. "I honestly don't know why I even thought I could make it work."

He took her hand, but she pulled it away. Her eyebrows knitted together, and her lips were set in a hard line. "We're alone and don't have to pretend."

"I'm not. I do care." Just because he needed a second to think about things didn't mean he didn't care. "I really do."

"No, you don't. You care about my business. You care about a potential investment. That's all." She began picking up the papers surrounding her. "We both know I'm wasting my time and money, but for the life of me, giving up just makes me want to puke."

He didn't think that at all. "That's not true, and you know it."

"Really? So I'm supposed to trust you, but you can't offer me the same?" She finished stacking the papers and set them on the nightstand. "That's not how it works."

Hunter felt gut-punched. "It's not that I don't trust you." He did trust her. It was just that...he hadn't wanted her to know about the money. How could he know she wanted him, just him, if she knew about it?

"Right."

"That's the truth." But even as he said it, he could hear the doubt in his own voice. If he were honest, it went beyond his doubts about her interest in him. Reagan finding out about the money bugged him, and he didn't know how to make it stop.

She glared at him, took a deep breath, and said, "I just wish I hadn't spent the money you gave me for Black Friday. If I could take the gifts back without making your family suspicious, I'd return everything."

"Reagan—"

Holding her hand up, she stopped him. She pinched the bridge of her nose. "You know what? Things worked better when you were on your side and I was on mine."

He nodded, unable to give a reason why it didn't have to be that way. "All right, I can respect that." As much as it bothered him that she knew about his money, this upset him even more.

Taking her hand again, he said, "Listen, you have

every right to be angry with me right now. I accept that, but I know some roofers on Tybee, and one owes me a favor. Would you be upset if I had them work on it?"

For a moment, she seemed to weigh his proposal, and then her body sagged. "I want to refuse, but…I can't see how I can make all of the repairs. I hate it. I don't want your money. If I could get back to the island, I would have already gone home."

Man, he'd messed things up good and proper. "I know, but with the evacuation order still in place, you can't. There's no power to the island and nowhere to stay even if you could get back on the island. Christmas is coming. Can we call a momentary truce?"

Just as he was beginning to think she'd tell him to go jump in the lake, she sighed. "Yeah, but from this point forward, I'm pretending."

"I know," he said and stood. "I'd like to take care of the roof, okay? I'll call my friend, use the favor he owes me, and have the bed and breakfast first on the list. No strings attached, just…because I want to."

Reagan nodded, drawing her knees to her chest and laying her head on them. "Okay, but I'm not taking any more of your money. I'll figure out a way to pay you back."

That wasn't a response from someone who was out

for his money, and it made him want to help her more, to make it right. "I don't doubt that, but there's no need." With that, he left her and walked out of the room, shutting the door behind him.

Hunter raked his hand through his hair. Two battles were waging. On one side, he missed Reagan. On the other side, he didn't want to get hurt. Both were giving him a headache, and both were equally valid—at least, in his mind.

His mom appeared at the top of the steps, bundled in jeans and a thick coat, and hooked a finger for him to follow her. He knitted his eyebrows together and headed her way. When he reached her, he said, "Is something wrong?"

She lifted one lone eyebrow and gave him one of her signature mom looks: *You and I are about to have a talk.* It was the one she reserved for when they'd really messed up, she knew it, and there was no getting out of it. Lumps were coming, and the only thing to be discussed was the force with which they were applied.

He followed her until they were outside on the porch.

She turned to him. "Park it," she said, pointing to the rocking chair.

Based on the tone of her voice, his rear was going

to be leather by the time she got done with him. "Yes, ma'am."

She pulled one of the other rockers closer and set it across from him. "You must think I'm pretty stupid."

What on earth was this kind of chewing? "I do not." This conversation was starting off horrible.

"Did you really think you could lie to me?"

His eyes widened. "Uh."

Her lips pinched together, and she leaned forward on her elbows, staring at him. It was worse than a police interrogation, but he wasn't a kid anymore. He wasn't giving up anything voluntarily.

Minute after minute, the staring contest went on. If it weren't so chilly, sweat would've been dripping down his face. He shifted in his seat, and the unease grew until he blurted, "Fine. I'm not really engaged to her."

His mom smiled. "Want to know how long I've known that?"

"Uh." Really? Again? Apparently, when he was in Caprock Canyon, his vocabulary took a vacation.

"Since the second I met her." She enunciated each word.

Hunter's jaw dropped. "No way."

She laughed. "Son, there is no chance you'd be engaged to a woman like that and take this long to introduce us to her. I don't know what the details are or how this arrangement came about, but I do know it's fake."

He slowly let out a breath he was holding. "Mom."

"I like her. You do too." A smile stretched on her lips. "Why do you think I told her about the lottery?"

"What?" He scoffed. "Why would you do that?"

"Because you boys use that money like a shield, holding it up so no one can get close. I get it. You don't want to be used and abused. That's understandable, but that young woman upstairs is too kind to be like that." His mom sat back in the chair. "You should have seen the look on her face when I told her. That poor thing had no idea what to do with the information."

His mom knew the whole time, and she *did* tell Reagan about the lottery. "Mom, why would you do that?"

"Because I wanted to be sure I was right. If she'd already known about the money, the color wouldn't have drained from her face, and it did. With the kind of tan she's got, it was like a white flag flying in a tornado." His mom chuckled. "And I also know she told you she knew."

Hunter blinked, trying to process everything. "How do you know she told me?"

"Honey, you don't go from smiles and winks to

cold fish for no reason. Why do you think I'm telling you this?" She crossed her arms over her chest and shook her head. "That poor girl is hurting. She's trying not to show it, but you can feel it in her spirit."

Nodding, he slouched in his seat and palmed his forehead. He couldn't refute it. He'd seen the look in her eyes. She was heartbroken, still trying to keep going, and her light was going dim. "I know. I told her I'd get her roof fixed."

His mom rolled her eyes. "Hunter, you can't fix this with money. That's what messed it up to start with." She shook her head and stood, stopping next to his rocker. "With the little bit I've learned, Reagan has been on her own most of her life. Reagan needs *you*. She needs a hand to hold, a shoulder to cry on, and most of all, she needs someone who won't bail the first chance they get." She patted him on the shoulder and left him alone on the porch.

The second Reagan told him she knew about the money and how she'd found out about it, he should have just believed her. Why *hadn't* he just trusted her? She had a list of people who'd let her down, and he was no better. Now, how was he going to make it up to her? What could he do to show he was sincere? Not things, that's for sure.

Man, he'd messed up so bad. And things had been going so well.

He rubbed his face with his hands and stood. Hopefully, she didn't hate him so much she was unwilling to hear his apology. He had a sinking feeling she did, but for once, he'd show her someone was willing to fight for her.

CHAPTER 16

Reagan groaned and walked to her bedroom door. The West-Fredericks Christmas Eve traditions would start in a few hours, and she wasn't ready yet. It had been over two weeks with Hunter trying to talk to her, but she wasn't ready to deal with him. Why was it that when *he* needed time to think, that's just how it was? But her? Oh, no. No one could ever give her the space she needed.

If it weren't for the hurricane, she'd have already gone back home, but according to Naomi and Kaylee, no one was being allowed back yet. Crews were still working on getting the electricity back to the island because of downed trees hitting power lines. Add to that, hotels even as far as four hours away were booked solid.

She whipped the door open. "Hunter, I'm—" She stopped short. "Uh, hi, Carrie Anne."

"Hi, I was wondering if you'd take a walk with me. I promise I asked others and this isn't a sly move. I just need a little fresh air." Hunter's sister smiled.

How could Reagan refuse that? Especially when she liked Carrie Anne. That girl had her brothers running scared, and it was hysterically funny to see four grown men cower in fear of someone who barely weighed a buck-twenty.

"You know what? I'd really like that." Reagan moved to get her coat.

"Oh, honey, this is West Texas. You can blink and the weather's changed. You don't really need a coat today. Do you have a sweater?"

Reagan shook her head. "Um." She did, but it was ratty. Money for clothes wasn't a luxury she had.

Carrie Anne waved for her to follow. "Come on, sister. I've got plenty."

"Okay." Reagan chuckled, and they walked to the room she shared with Israel.

Carrie Anne pulled the closet doors open and turned to Reagan. "Anything I have is yours, so take your pick."

Reagan smiled. "Uh, are you sure?"

"Sure, I'm sure." She tilted her head. "I bet you'd look great in a deep green or something like that. I love the color, but it makes me look like a bleached pickle with blonde hair." Carrie Anne dug through the clothes and pulled out two hands full of clothes. "If you like these, take them. My husband will love you."

Laughing, Reagan followed her to the bed where she laid out a couple of sweaters, a cardigan, and some shirts. Carrie Anne held them against herself and said, "See? Awful. And I don't tan. I burn, just burn to a fried crisp." Hunter's sister eyed her. "I bet you tan just thinking about the sun, don'tcha?"

"Kinda." Reagan snorted and quickly covered her mouth with her hand.

"I knew it." She smiled.

Reagan loved every one of the pieces Carrie Anne had chosen. They were cute, clean, and, most of all, new. She wasn't sure how long it had been since she'd bought new clothes. She'd spent all of the Black Friday money on Hunter and his family rather than herself. "Are you sure you're okay giving these things to me? Gabby might be able to wear them."

Carrie Anne's eyebrows reached her hairline. "She hates this color. Likes it on me, but she won't touch it with a ten-foot pole."

“Thank you,” Reagan said and picked up a soft chenille sweater, slipping it on. She ran her hand down the arm and sighed. “It’s so soft. I love it.”

“Well, let’s go for that walk, and when we get back, we’ll put the rest in your room.”

“Okay. That sounds good to me.”

Carrie Anne hooked her arm in Reagan’s, and they talked as they walked until they hit the front steps. Reagan took a deep breath and nearly melted. It was much warmer than it had been; there was a crisp, clean scent in the air; and it was so quiet. Normally, she would have missed the ocean, but right then, the silence was soothing.

“Do you have a directional preference?” Carrie Anne asked, dropping her arm from Reagan’s.

“Nope, I’m with you.”

“All right, then.” Carrie Anne smiled.

They got to the end of the drive and turned left. For a good stretch, they just walked. Carrie Anne didn’t ask any questions, and Reagan didn’t try to start small talk. She hadn’t realized just how much she’d needed to feel that someone was beside her. Someone not dragging her along but letting her go at her own pace.

“Feeling better?” Carrie Anne asked and glanced at Reagan.

She nodded. "Actually, yeah."

With a nod, Carrie Anne said, "I thought you needed it. I'm sorry about your bed and breakfast. I can't imagine how that hurts."

"Yeah, me too. Don't tell Hunter, but he has no idea how grateful I am that he's helping with the roof." Not just the roof, but other little things he'd failed to mention without asking her. It was really sweet because she'd been so angry with him, and there he was, being even sweeter. "I wish I didn't need the help."

Carrie Anne waved her off. "Oh, everyone needs help sometimes."

Reagan balled her fists in the sweater and hugged herself. "I know, but I seem to need it all the time."

"Yeah, my grandpa, Grandma Jo's husband, said people go through seasons. Sometimes, the person going through the hardship isn't going through it for them. Sometimes they're going through it for someone else who needs it." Carrie Anne sighed. "I always said it didn't seem fair, and, believe me, it's never easy. This was when I got my braces and had to wear headgear for two whole years...starting in seventh grade. I had a crush on Tex Carter. Oh, girl, I thought he'd hung the moon and stars."

"What happened?" asked Reagan.

"That little turkey started making fun of me the second the bell rang. One day I lost it and popped him square on the nose. Of course, I was the one who got in trouble. I was hurt and mad and sad and every other emotion you could imagine. Mom and Dad chewed me raw, and I was grounded for what felt like an eternity at the time." Carrie Anne chuckled. "One of my punishments was to pull weeds from my grandparents' flower beds, and my grandpa sat right there with me while I pulled them. We'd talk and talk when I did that."

Reagan glanced at her. "How long was your punishment?"

"Oh, six weeks, but I liked talking to my grandpa. After all the weeds were gone, I'd pretend to pull them, and he'd sit outside with me. He turned it into our special thing, and I loved it. I learned so much from him." Carrie Anne rubbed her eyes, and Reagan smiled. "I'm not misty-eyed. It's dirt." She laughed.

"Sure." Reagan worked to keep the smile hidden and cleared her throat. "That sounds like a good memory. My family has owned that bed and breakfast for generations. My great-great-grandparents opened it, and that's all she wrote." Reagan's thoughts whirled with memories of her family, how they worked and toiled for that bed and breakfast. "I don't remember having time like that. As soon as I learned to cook, I was put in the kitchen."

Carrie Anne nodded and looked at her. "Reagan, do you want to own that bed and breakfast? I mean, when you took over, did you ever question it?"

Mid-stride, Reagan stopped dead. That had never been a question. It was just what happened. When her parents considered retiring, she was the one going to take it over. There was nothing else presented. No options. "No. I mean, no, I was never asked. I do love it, but sometimes, I get so tired of it. But it's all I've ever known. Everything I am. My very being is attached to that house."

Reagan inhaled a ragged breath and braced her hands on her knees. She'd never even considered that there could be another option. It was a multiple-choice question, and all she'd seen was one answer. Before she knew it, tears were gushing.

Carrie Anne wrapped her arms around Reagan. "I'm so sorry. I wasn't trying to upset you. Oh, I feel awful."

Her insides were so tangled it was making her stomach hurt. What was she going to do now? Her answer to running the bed and breakfast was always the same: she loved it. But did she? "It's not your fault."

"You're not that bed and breakfast, though. You can

love something, feel immensely attached to it, but it's not you." Carrie Anne leaned back. "Can I ask what made you think you were?"

Shrugging, Reagan struggled to find the answer to the question. "I honestly don't know."

Nodding, Carrie Anne said, "I'm not saying you need to give up or anything, but maybe you should stop putting it first and yourself second."

Reagan blinked. How would she even do that? The concept was completely foreign. Hunter's sister was right, though. That bed and breakfast was always front and center, and she was the participation trophy no one wanted. That wasn't how it was supposed to be.

"Thank you," Reagan said. "What's funny is my two friends back home, Naomi and Kaylee, tried to get me to see that when I first mentioned I was going to take over for Mom and Dad. I've been so attached to that place. When someone was talking about it, they were talking about me. But I'm just me and nothing else."

Carrie Anne hugged her. "I think you're pretty awesome. Running a bed and breakfast has to be a lot of work." She pulled back. "I know I couldn't do it."

"I couldn't teach, so I think we're even." Reagan smiled, glad Carrie Anne was off for Christmas break. It hadn't occurred to Reagan how much she needed someone to talk to. Of course, she could have called Naomi or Kaylee, but to tell the truth, until this moment, she didn't know how she felt. Not really.

"You know, I'm gonna like having you as a sister." Carrie Anne dropped her arms. "I know you and Hunter have been frosty the last couple of weeks, but couples argue. I'm sure he did something moronic. Anyone tell you about Wyatt and how he and Gabby got together?"

"No." Reagan shook her head.

Hunter's sister hooked her arm in Reagan's, and they began walking again as she told the story. She'd been missing out on things like this. Everything revolved around the business, and at some point, she'd taken a back seat. She didn't even know when it had happened. Maybe that first day in the kitchen cooking? Could it have been before that?

All this time, she'd called herself a failure. Allowed all the negative things said to etch themselves onto her. She wasn't The Sandy Pelican. She was Reagan Loveless, and she was worth more than a beachfront bed and breakfast.

In a way, Hunter had been telling her the same thing. If nothing else, she'd thank him for that. That didn't mean she wasn't still upset with him, but he deserved thanks where it was due. The fate of the business was on shaky ground, but for the first time in her life, she was standing on solid rock.

CHAPTER 17

Normally, Christmas Eve would be relaxing for Hunter. The scent of spiced cider and fresh pine floating in the air along with the smell of Bandit's cinnamon rolls baking, fire flickering in the fireplace, everyone sitting around the tree, and the hum of conversation. That's what made it Christmas Eve.

A couple of years ago, the occasional beverage dumped in a lap would have been par for the course too, but now that Bear had the ranch house, there was elbow room for everyone.

Just before the festivities started, he leaned against the wall next to the stairs, waiting for Reagan to come down. She'd gone for a walk with his sister, and whatever they'd talked about had helped her, which made him especially grateful to Carrie Anne.

A deep breath caught his attention, and he looked up. Reagan stood on the second landing, staring at him. Whatever she was thinking was a mystery because her face was masked.

"Hey," he said.

"Hi."

She slowly descended the steps and stopped before reaching the bottom landing. "I love your sister."

He smiled. "She has her moments."

"I guess it's time to be engaged again?" The way her mouth turned down was an arrow to his heart.

He'd struggled with whether to tell her his mom knew. In the end, he'd decided not just yet. He was afraid she'd get on the next plane headed to Tybee, and he was desperate to right things between them. If he was wrong, he'd deal with the consequences.

Hunter held his hand out to her. His mom said he needed to show Reagan he was with her, and he'd taken that to heart. With that in mind, he was approaching the evening with a different attitude. "I guess it is."

She walked down the last two steps and slipped her hand into his. For a second, her entire demeanor was rigid and guarded.

"Reagan,—"

Holding her hand up, she stopped him. "I'm agreeing to a truce." She softened, and her gaze went to the floor. "I'm also big enough to offer thanks when and where it's warranted. I'm not The Sandy Pelican. We are two entirely different entities, and Carrie Anne helped me see that earlier."

"Good."

"But you started it. For that, I'm grateful." She lifted her gaze to his. "I'm not necessarily giving up at this point, but I know there's more than one way now. I have a right to choose which direction I go."

The light in her eyes was worth everything. "I don't think I had anything to do with that revelation, but I'm happy for the truce."

"And I want to say thank you for the roof, and all the other little things you managed to sneak in." She pointed a finger at him. "You thought I wouldn't get wind, but you were wrong. I'll be paying those back too."

Hunter rubbed his knuckles along his jaw as fire raced up his neck. "Uh."

"You need to work on your vocabulary when you're under stress. You've got a lot of *uh's* and not much else." She smiled. "On a serious note, despite how this may have started, I've enjoyed meeting your family."

"Is it against the rules to hug you?" he asked, hoping for the best and preparing for the worst.

Shaking her head, she stepped into him, tucking her hands in against his chest. He was pretty sure this was what his mom meant by needing him and not his money. He kissed the top of her head and rested his cheek against it.

"You keep stopping me from apologizing—"

She pulled back. "Hunter," she said, shaking her head.

He covered her mouth with his hand. "I'm sorry for overreacting about the money. It wasn't right to do that. I guess…I guess you weren't the only one in need of a revelation."

Holding his gaze, Reagan sighed and waited a few beats before taking his hand from her mouth. "Okay." As she leaned into him again, he wrapped his arms around her.

He'd enjoyed kissing her, but this, just being together, was more precious than the kissing. Not that he didn't want more of the kissing, but he liked this just as much.

Wyatt stepped out of the living room. "Come on, lovebirds. You're holding everything up." He grinned.

Reagan stepped back and looked at him. "I smell cinnamon rolls. If all this hugging has made me late and they're cold, the next time I make coffee..." Her lips turned up, and her eyes glinted with mischief. "Well, we'll just leave it there. That way, I can feign innocence."

Shaking his head, Hunter laughed. "Come on. Let's go find a seat."

Her fingers tangled in his without him even asking, and he could have fist-pumped the air. First a hug and now holding hands? They weren't huge victories, but he'd take them.

On their way to the living room, they stopped in the kitchen. Most of his family had already taken their share of the goodies, a cinnamon roll, and their choice of hot chocolate, cider, or milk. Once they were loaded up, they walked to the living room and took a spot out of the line of traffic near the back of the tree, setting their drinks on the floor.

When they got seated, Reagan eyed him. "Anxious for presents?"

"No, this is self-preservation." He smiled. "I learned the hard way to stay away from the traffic after one too many hot drinks were dumped on me."

Reagan covered her mouth with her hand and giggled.

He scoffed. "That's not funny."

That only made her laugh harder.

Balancing his plate with one hand, Hunter slipped his arm around her and pulled her closer. "It's not nice to laugh at someone."

"If you make me drop my cinnamon roll, I'm taking yours." She wrinkled her nose as she teased him.

He set his lips next to her ear. "You may not believe me, but I love hearing you laugh."

Her laugh died, and she straightened and looked into his eyes. It seemed as if she were debating how to respond. Leaning in, she said, "I don't think I've ever loved a smile as much as I love yours. It makes your eyes a lighter color."

The root of hope grew a little deeper, and the uncertainty he'd had before lessened. "Can we negotiate terms to move past the white flag?"

"Let's…let's take things as they come."

He pressed his lips to her forehead. "You're the boss."

A wide smile quirked on her lips, reaching all the way to her eyes. "That definitely gets me to the table."

Mr. Fredericks put his hands to his mouth. "Okay, it's time to start gifts. This year we're drawing names out of a hat. Remember, the smallest gift. No secret alliances are allowed," he said and eyed Josiah.

Hunter busted out laughing and looked at Reagan. "He was caught two Christmases ago talking to Wyatt."

Josiah grumbled. "I was not."

Carrie Anne leveled her eyes at him. "I heard you with my own ears, you dork."

"No, you didn't. I told you we were talking about something else."

Caroline gave a time-out signal. "Okay, you two, stop it." She shook her head. "Oil and water work better together than these two sometimes."

"See why I'm glad you came?" Hunter asked Reagan just above a whisper.

"I love it. I wish I'd had this when I was growing up." The corners of her mouth were lifted slightly as her gaze met his. "This is the best Christmas Eve I've ever had."

In an instant, he was seeing Christmas futures with her snuggled next to him. That laughter that made his heart beat to its rhythm. There was no one else he could ever see filling that spot. He wanted her to know how he felt, but first she needed to finally hear him out about how wrong he'd been to not trust her. That discussion was long overdue but not something he wanted to have in front of his entire family.

The gifts were barely finished being opened when Hunter took Reagan's hand and stood, pulling her up with him. Without saying a word, he led her through the house to the study. When they stepped inside, he shut the door and turned to her.

"What's going on?" she asked.

"I owe you an apology that's more than a few sentences long."

She opened her mouth like she was going to stop him and then closed it, nodding. "Okay."

Holding her gaze, he took a deep breath and let it out slowly. This was it. What they had currently was a start, but he wanted the solid ground back that they'd had before he'd been so stupid. "I had a conversation with my mom. She told me she was the one who told you."

Crossing her arms over her chest, Reagan said, "I told you she did."

"I know, and I should have believed you the second you said it."

"Why didn't you?"

He'd been chewing on that since his conversation with his mom. It was more than just using the money as a shield. "Having so much money has been a curse in some ways. It's made me suspicious of everyone since so many people see me differently because of it." If they were going to have a relationship, he needed to be completely honest with her. "For a second, I was afraid you had known all along and were using it against me as far as the bed and breakfast went, but I knew in my heart that wasn't true."

He stepped closer and took her hands. "I'm sorry I doubted you. You've never once given me reason to believe you're like that." He sighed. "All my life I've wanted to be successful and loved for who I am, and some may see winning that money as a success, but I wanted to achieve it in an honorable, self-made way. I—"

"And you have."

"I hope so, but when I heard you knew about the money, it…I don't know, those fears just sank their hooks in me. I didn't want you to see me in that way. I don't even touch the lottery money if I can help it; my business pays the bills. Your opinion is the only one that matters anymore, and I hated that it might be swayed when you heard about the money."

She blinked. "*My* opinion?"

"Yes, your opinion. I care about you." It was so much more than care, but with them just starting to get along, he didn't want to push things. "I could be the most successful person in the world, and if you didn't think so, none of it would matter. The idea that you could see all the work I've done summed up in dollar bills bothered me."

Until that moment, he'd felt the words, but hearing them cemented the reason why it had bothered him so much. Reagan having faith in him meant the world to him, and he wanted that faith attached to him as a person and not money.

She took his face in her hands. "Hunter, you're more than a bank account. At least, to me you are. You're funny and kind and caring." She hugged him around the neck.

Wrapping his arms around her, he touched his forehead to hers. "Will you forgive me?"

She squeezed tighter. "Yes. Thank you for giving me the space I needed in the meantime."

Immediately, a heavy weight fell from his shoulders. He could handle years and years of just this: holding on to each other, facing their fears and doubts together. A partner in life and love and home. For the first time that he could remember, he felt at peace with himself.

CHAPTER 18

The sun wasn't even up yet on Christmas morning, and Reagan was positive she'd be the only person in the kitchen. She'd had a fitful night of sleep, and instead of just lying there, she'd decided to make herself some coffee. As she reached the kitchen, she stopped short, finding King and Caroline sitting at the bar, talking.

"Good morning, Reagan," King said. "Not to be selfish, but I'm relieved you're here. Caroline threatened me by offering to make me coffee."

Caroline swatted him on the arm with the back of her hand. "I've already admitted it tasted like dirt, didn't I? I wasn't trying to poison you, you old codger."

King snickered and shushed her. "People are still sleeping."

They were so cute. Reagan had never caught her parents being like that. Then again, her parents were always working, and now that she had a better look at the finances, they were probably always under stress from fear of the next big disaster.

Reagan rolled her lips in, trying not to laugh. Suddenly, she had a goal added to her list: to find herself sitting in the kitchen, enjoying the person she considered her best friend. What really kicked her in the stomach was that Hunter was the only person she could see filling that empty spot anymore.

She'd fallen in love with him. As ticked as she'd been, it was the absolute truest thing she'd ever felt. The realization was a lightning bolt hitting her heart so hard it nearly stopped. It made perfect sense, though. That's why it had hurt her so badly that he didn't trust her. Why she'd lashed out at him too. It was all an effort to protect herself.

"Do you mind making coffee, Reagan? You are absolutely not obligated if you don't want to," King said.

Lifting her gaze to his, she smiled. "No, I don't mind. That's what I came down for anyway." Then a little thought danced through her head. What would it be like to call Hunter's family hers? She shook the thought away. Good grief, talk about jumping the gun.

Caroline stood and stretched. "I think I'm going to run upstairs and shower really quick. I'm feeling sticky from last night." She pushed on King's back with her hand. "All that room, and you just had to spill cold hot chocolate on me. I cleaned it off, but I'm still feeling gross."

King shrugged. "I didn't anticipate you standing the very moment I decided to take our stuff to the sink. You headbutted me."

"I should have made you coffee and made ya drink it." She winked and kissed him on the cheek.

"Go take your shower, my love. I'll have the cream and sugar on the counter for you when you get back." He blew her a kiss as she sauntered out of the kitchen.

He turned to Reagan. "I give her grief, but, man, I love her. Just so happens, she's one hot chick too. I'm pretty sure I'm the luckiest guy on the planet."

Reagan loved the way they loved each other. It wasn't stuffy or toned down when someone else was around. Plus, to her, it was the sweetest thing a man could say about his wife. Was it possible this was a glimpse for her future?

Inwardly, she groaned. Her brain had to give it a rest. While she got the coffee going, she said, "Last night was more fun than I've ever had on a Christmas Eve. I love your traditions."

It had been the most fun and a challenge to find the smallest gift they could find to go under the tree. They'd told her about it on their trip to Amarillo on Black Friday, but she hadn't truly understood they meant business.

She'd loved everything about the evening. The cinnamon rolls were soft and gooey and glazy. Hers were pretty good, but Bandit was a master. Everything added up to memories that lasted.

In all her life, she'd never experienced anything like it. The deep connections, the stories that never ran out, and the way they teased and picked on each other. If nothing else, at the end of the evening, she found herself wanting to find a way to return each Christmas.

Hunter's dad leaned forward with his arms on the counter. "Caroline told me a few things about you. I've got plenty of time, and I'd love to hear it from you." He smiled.

Now Reagan understood where Hunter got his charm. "Well, I grew up on Tybee Island." While the coffee started brewing, she crossed her arms over her chest and leaned her hip against the edge of the counter.

It was hard not to compare her parents to Hunter's, but they'd led such different lives. Her parents weren't bad parents; they were busy parents. And now that she was running the bed and breakfast, it was easier to put herself in their shoes.

Before she knew it, she was drinking hot coffee and giving King an entire memoir's worth of her life story. The neatest and best thing was that not once did he seem hurried or bored. Honestly, that was one of the things she liked about Hunter.

Cripes. Oh, she was done for. She wasn't in love with Hunter; she was over-the-moon, hold-me-forever in love with him. It was the foot-pop moment in *The Princess Diaries*. He was her…cowboy prince who made her feel whole.

"So, I guess my grands are gonna be all the way in Georgia, huh?"

Good thing she didn't have coffee in her mouth or he'd have a face full. She was *not* prepared for that little gem of a question. "Uh." Vocabulary gone. Hunter had infected her.

King chuckled. "I did the same thing to Israel. At least you managed to form some kind of a word."

She shook her head. "Yep. Hunter doesn't fall far from the tree." And she was glad because when she was old and gray, she wanted her husband to look at her the way King had looked at Caroline.

Again, she caught herself wanting Hunter to fill all the niches of her life. Good grief, she needed to stop.

"There's a rumor that my son roped you into pretending to be engaged to him." He sat back and smiled. "My gut tells me my source is right, but I also see the way my boy looks at you. If that's not smitten, I don't know what is." He waggled a finger at her. "And you, young lady, are just the kind of woman to keep him on his toes. So, I won't dwell on the rumor." He leaned forward. "I just hope the engagement is true someday." He leaned back.

Suddenly, Reagan had a deep understanding of being blindsided. The kind where the car drives off with half the bumper and the victim is left holding their latte, wondering what just happened. Her mouth was dry and her mind devoid of any comeback that could be believed.

"Okay, I'm ready for some coffee. Sorry that took so long, but once I got in, I didn't want to get out. Good thing Bear installed those tankless water heaters. I'd have had a mob after me," Caroline said as she walked into the kitchen.

King gave Reagan a quick wink and kissed Caroline on the cheek as he stood. "Let me get that cream and sugar, darlin'. Time got away from me." He placed his hand on her shoulder, and she smiled up at him.

"Thank you, sweetheart." Caroline looked straight at Reagan. "That coffee smells delicious. I caught wind of it upstairs. I don't think we'll be alone down here for long."

"Let me get you some coffee," Reagan said, her voice a little on the squeaky side.

King knew they weren't engaged, and if he knew, Caroline knew. When had Caroline figured it out? They'd been kissy, affectionate. Sure, they'd had a disagreement—a big one—but all couples had those. Should Reagan acknowledge that they knew? This was a playbook she was wholly unfamiliar with.

Had they told Hunter that they knew? No, he'd have said something for sure. Or would he have? She had been really upset with him, and it wasn't like she had anywhere to go until the island was open for residents to return. Which, if he'd told her, she would have wanted to go home, even if she didn't have a roof over her head. Staying at the ranch would have made her feel awkward.

For now, she'd keep the information to herself. They'd spend Christmas enjoying her family and maybe trying to figure out what this thing between them was. All she knew was that she loved him. That's where negotiations could start.

CHAPTER 19

By noon, most of Hunter's family was ready to open gifts. They'd huddled around in the kitchen talking for a while, long enough to require several pots of Reagan's coffee. She'd given Bandit some tips, but it just wasn't the same.

Currently, they were in the middle of unwrapping gifts. What they typically did was hand them all out, and then they'd each take turns opening them so everyone could see what they got. Hunter couldn't remember when that tradition had started, which meant it was much older than him.

They'd gone several rounds and were stopped at him again. This last pass would be the final gift to unwrap. He picked up the one from Reagan which he'd saved until now. He wondered what she could have possibly gotten him. At least she'd gone shopping before she was mad at him. There would've been no telling what it was otherwise.

"Are you going to stare at it or open it?" asked Bear.

"Shut up," Hunter grumbled.

He pulled the wrapping off and opened the little box. A smile spread on his lips. "Dog training lessons?"

Reagan shrugged. "I thought they might come in handy one day."

Yeah, and maybe their dog would be the ring bearer at their wedding. His heart skipped a beat at the thought. It was as clear a picture as he'd ever had. Hunter walking down the aisle toward Reagan, and the beginning of a life with someone he respected and loved.

Hunter put his arm around her and kissed her forehead. "Thank you." He'd unwrapped two gifts, and the one he loved most was her.

"You're welcome."

Gabby was next and the last person to open the final gift. She picked up what looked to be a t-shirt-sized gift box.

"Gabby?" Wyatt asked. "No *to* or *from*?"

Shrugging, she grinned and unwrapped it, pulled the top off the box, and then began unfolding what looked like a poster. She held it up, and the room fell silent. On the poster, there was a pink and blue onesie with a due date.

Wyatt turned to her. "Really?"

She nodded. "Yeah."

"Pregnant?" A range of emotion played on Wyatt's face, from shock to awe to joy.

Their mom's breath caught, and her hand went to her mouth. She looked from Gabby to Pauline, Gabby's mother. "Did you know?"

Pauline shook her head as tears began streaming down her cheeks. "No."

"They got us a baby for Christmas," his mom said, choking out the words.

As Wyatt kissed his wife, the entire family broke into a ruckus of everything from congratulations to flat-out bawling from the soon-to-be grandmas.

Hunter looked at Reagan, and their eyes locked. He was going to be an uncle, and he never wanted anything more than for her to be an aunt. He loved her and wanted her and a life with her. Hopefully, she was thinking the same thing.

CHAPTER 20

Since Christmas, things between Reagan and Hunter had been different. Good, but not what they'd been before their date and better than it was Christmas Eve. They seemed to have an unspoken agreement on what direction they were headed. Of course, they'd only spent a little time together.

Residents were now being allowed back onto the island to see how their homes had fared through the hurricane. Hunter's partner, Stone, had somehow managed to be one of the first to return. He'd called and used Facetime to let her see it. Her home had sustained some damage, but thankfully, not as much as she'd feared.

Hunter had convinced her to stay in Caprock Canyon while he got a crew working on it. That way she'd have a place to stay once they got back. Depending on how his hotel fared, maybe he'd have a place too.

A situation had come up with one of the flip houses, and with the way Hunter had secluded himself, it must have been bad. He hadn't seemed overly stressed, but she'd also given him space to deal with the problem.

It worked out well since the women of the family decided Gabby needed some girl time and they'd gone to Amarillo on New Year's Eve. Reagan was pretty sure it was an excuse for Caroline, Pauline, and Carrie Anne to buy baby clothes. This first grandchild was going to be set for life based on the number of onesies they'd purchased. Reagan had to admit part of her envied Gabby. This family, the way they went whole-hog loving each other…Reagan couldn't see anyone not wanting to be part of it.

Only a few hours ago they had returned, and now they were getting ready to watch some fireworks. Apparently, the year before there had been a wedding and an engagement. Instead of taking a chance something would catch fire, they'd held off on them.

Now dressed, Reagan wanted to find Hunter. A phone call here and there wasn't the same thing as being held in his arms. As she reached the study, she could hear him talking to someone. Just as she'd decided to turn around, she heard him say something about The Sandy Pelican.

Her heart rate double as she crept closer, trying to hear what was being said. Part of her wanted to trust him, but the other part, the one still trying to figure out where the bed and breakfast fit in her life, wanted to know what was being said.

She peeked through the crack in the door and found Hunter with his back to her and the phone to his ear.

"Yeah, go ahead and gut the last two bedrooms. There's no point in updating one room and not the others," Hunter said.

Reagan smiled. Not long ago, she would have been furious, but things had changed. Hunter helping her wasn't him saying she wasn't good enough. It was saying he cared about her and the things that mattered to her.

"I know, Stone...Well, I'm going to have it fixed up and then see about buying it...No, she has no idea...I guess I charmed it out of her." He laughed.

Reagan's pulse raced faster as she leaned her back against the wall. She had to be hearing things wrong. Hunter wouldn't do that to her. But then again, he'd wanted the bed and breakfast. Badly. Enough that he'd said he'd wait her out because he knew it would fail.

He also knew she didn't have the funds to keep it going for more than a year. With the damage from the hurricane affecting tourism, it would take well over a year to bounce back.

She put her hand over her heart and felt the shatter as it happened. His parents knew they were faking it. All this time, what if this was his plan? To get her defenses down and make her think he cared about her, only to fix the place up under the guise of helping? That way, when she ran out of money, all he'd have to do is buy and move in.

Pushing off the wall, Reagan made her way back to her room, a numbness spreading from her heart and encompassing her. He'd used her, lied to her, and she'd fallen for all of it. Fallen in love with him. How could someone with a family so incredible be so ruthless and cruel?

Was that why he wanted to stay in Georgia? So they wouldn't know what kind of person they'd raised? That seemed to be the only way she could explain it.

After locking the door to her room, she curled up on her bed, wondering how she was going to survive the next two days. They'd planned to leave the day after tomorrow. A whole forty-eight hours with a man who made her physically ill. How was she going to do it?

A knock came from her door. "Hey, Reagan, the fireworks are about to start," Carrie Anne called through the door.

Reagan sat up and took a deep breath, and as the numbness subsided, anger took its place. If Hunter could keep up pretenses, she could too. Plus, she loved his family. They were good people, and she had no doubts they had no idea who Hunter truly was.

She stood, squared her shoulders, and walked to the door. As she unlocked it, she plastered a smile on her face and opened it. "Hey, I'm ready."

"I'm ready for some sweet iced tea, some Texas chocolate sheet cake, and a sky filled with colors. How about you?" His sister's smile was wide and bright.

"I'm absolutely ready for it, especially that cake. It sounds delicious. I may have to put it on the menu at The Sandy Pelican." She grinned.

Two days. She could do anything for two days. When they got back to Tybee, she'd be ready for war. He'd never see it coming.

CHAPTER 21

The fireworks display going on was incredible, and the night sky was lit with an array of colors. Not only had Bear set it all up, but he'd even gone so far as to get outdoor seating. Hunter suspected there'd be a movie screen at some point. With the ranch being so far away from a major city, entertainment was a little sparse.

The past week when Hunter wasn't working on selling his share of the business, he was helping his brother herd the cattle away from the house. A couple of nights, they'd even camped out in the pasture so they could get done in time for New Year's Eve. No one wanted to take a chance on them getting spooked and hurting themselves because of the noise. Plus, it was just good stewardship to take care of the animals the right way.

Hunter leaned over to Reagan who was sitting to his left. "This is pretty good, huh?"

"It's beautiful." Her tone seemed laced with iciness.

"Have I done something wrong?" he asked.

She shook her head, but her body language screamed in disagreement.

Hunter studied her a second. What could he have done? They hadn't even seen much of each other. As soon as he'd had the chance, he'd called Stone to discuss Hunter's desire to retire from flipping. It had never crossed his mind that Stone didn't want to be full owner, but once Hunter knew that, they came up with a different plan.

Together, they'd approached Ryan with the idea that he could purchase Hunter's half. Since the man had been with West Stone Renovations for three years, he knew the business well enough that he could help Stone. What he didn't know, Stone could teach him. It had been the best solution for all of them.

Once that was taken care of, Hunter had contacted the bank about the bed and breakfast. His plan was to have the house completely done before they returned to the island. He'd wanted to surprise her and then tell her he loved her. To his thinking, it would show he wanted her more than he wanted anything. Once he did that, he would offer to take care of the note as well.

"Reagan, is this about the money issue again? I'm sorry I hurt you when you admitted to knowing about the lottery. I should've...I should have handled it better. I know you well enough to know you'd never have been that kind of person." More than anything, he wished he could walk back in time and do things so much different. She'd said she'd forgiven him, but maybe it hadn't been as easy as she'd thought.

She turned to him, shot him a smile, and kissed his cheek. "I appreciate the apology, but nothing's wrong."

It all felt off. Reagan was warm and gentle and caring, and what he saw was an imitation of the woman he knew she was. "Really? Because if I've done something else, just tell me. Whatever it is, we can work it out."

Her body softened against him. "I'm sorry. I guess I'm just worried about returning to the island. I know I have a lot of work to do to get the word out that The Sandy Pelican is ready for reservations."

Yeah, he could see that being something to plague her mind. He started to speak, but she touched his lips with her fingers. "It's okay. Everything is fine. Let's just watch the fireworks. I think I need another piece of cake, though. Want me to get you one while I'm up?"

"No, I'm okay for now."

She stood, bent down, and gave him a small kiss on the lips. "I'll be right back."

Hunter watched her walk away, and in his gut, he knew something was wrong. But maybe he was just reading into it. The last couple of months had been a roller coaster. Being gone so long would be a little nerve-wracking.

For a second, he wondered if he should just tell her what he'd planned, but he really wanted it to be something between the two of them. He'd always been taught that talk was cheap, and he wanted her to see that he had action to back up what he was saying.

He loved her. He loved the things that mattered to her. More than anything, he wanted her to feel like she had a choice in whether she kept The Sandy Pelican or not. With it paid off, she'd be given the chance to do that. A choice she should have had from the very beginning.

To him, loving her was standing beside her, holding her hand, and, hopefully, deciding together where they wanted to be. He just needed to relax. When they got back to Tybee, everything would be okay.

CHAPTER 22

Numbness had turned to anger, and anger had turned to fury. The return trip to Tybee Island was almost more than Reagan could handle. Being in the same airspace with Hunter was making her physically ill. He'd yet to break character, though, and she was just waiting for him to show his true colors.

Cutting the engine to the truck when they finally reached the bed and breakfast, he turned to her and smiled. "I'd missed my family, but I have to admit, it's good to be back. I never thought I'd think of a little island in Georgia as home."

She nodded as she looked her home over. It looked nearly brand new. It was gorgeous, and had she not overheard him saying he wanted to buy the place, she'd have thought he'd done it for her. "Yep. It's good to be back."

"I know you keep saying nothing is wrong, but I'm getting the distinct feeling I've done something, and I don't know what it is. But—"

Still going. She'd have thought the act would be old by now. She opened the door and hopped out. He could keep playing, but she'd run out of patience at this point. Pulling open the back door, she grabbed her luggage. Before she could shut it, he was out of the truck and rounding the back.

"Reagan, what is going on? What have I done to make you so mad?"

She slammed the back door closed and stared up at him, mystified that he could still be acting like nothing was wrong. The only thing she could figure was that he'd planned to whammy her good after they got back.

Grabbing the handle of her luggage, she began walking away from him, but he hurried and stepped in front of her. "What did I do?"

She let go of the handle and crossed her arms over her chest. "I'm just some stupid, easily fooled..." She stopped as tears blurred her vision. She loved this man, and no matter what he'd done to her, her heart just couldn't believe he'd betray her like he was. "I heard you talking to someone. You were getting

The Sandy Pelican all jazzed up…so you could buy it."

"That's not—"

"It's exactly in line with what you said the last time you offered to buy the place. 'I'll just wait you out and let the bank foreclose on you.' Then you'd just slide on in and take it."

He raked his hand through his hair, set his hands on his hips, and cast his gaze to the ground. Like he had a reason to be frustrated and upset. She wasn't trying to rip his business away from him.

Lifting his gaze to hers, he asked, "Do you really believe that? After everything, you think I'm like that?"

"I heard you, Hunter, and it's not exactly a secret that you wanted to buy the place. That hurricane just gave you the excuse to fix it up and 'charm me out of it.' I know I can't last until the tourism starts back up. We both know it'll take a while for the island bounce back."

His eyebrows knitted together, and he nodded. "Well, I guess you have me all figured out, then."

Man, he was good. For a split-second, she caught herself doubting what she'd heard, but there was no misunderstanding it. He'd said he was buying the place. Those were his words. He'd charmed her out of it.

"I guess I do. Unless you have a different explanation."

"No," he said softly. "I don't. Let me get the rest of what I owe you."

"Oh, no. I don't want anything else from you. I don't care if I have to bus tables until I'm eighty—I'm paying you back." How could he act like he was the one hurting when it was he who had betrayed her?

He swallowed hard and stepped aside. "Okay. I guess…well, I guess…" He let the sentence trail off and strode back to his pickup, leaving her watching him pull away.

The tears slid down her cheeks, and part of her wanted to go chasing after him. She wasn't desperate, though. He'd offered no explanation for what she'd heard. If there had been one, he would have said something.

When the truck pulled out of the driveway, she caught the handle of her luggage and slowly trudged inside. At one time, it would have felt wonderful to come home. Now, it felt more like a noose. Maybe she just needed to let him have it, pull up stakes, and find another place to call home. This one sure didn't feel like it anymore.

CHAPTER 23

After dropping Reagan off at the bed and breakfast, Hunter had returned to Caprock Canyon, unsure he'd ever be able to step foot on that island again. The whole way there, he'd practiced telling her he loved her and then showing her that the house was hers, free and clear.

Instead, she'd accused him of trying to swipe it from under her. If she could think that way about him now, after all the time they'd spent together, then it never would have worked between them anyway. With zero trust, a relationship was doomed to fail from the beginning.

Sure, she could have questioned him at the beginning, but things had been good between them. He'd apologized for being stupid that night, had opened up to her more than he had with anyone, and yet, she still expected him to be so low as to try to steal her home from her.

Sleeping had become near impossible. So much so that the last week, he'd found himself on the front porch before the sun rose. It was cold, but as empty as he felt, it didn't really bother him.

The door opened, and his mom stepped out with a cup in each hand. As she passed him, she handed him one. He looked at it.

"No, I didn't make it," she grumbled.

A grunt of a laugh came from his throat. "Okay."

For a while, they sat in silence. So far, no one had really gone beyond asking what happened. His replies had been short on detail and long on snappy. He didn't want to talk about it, especially not at length.

"Hunter, you've been home over a week now. I've given you space, watched you grow sullen, and now, I'm asking you to tell me what happened," she said as she finished her coffee and set the mug next to her rocker. "If you snap at me like you did the first day you got here, I'm going to go get your daddy and prove that a thirty-four-year-old man can, in fact, get his rear end paddled for sassing his momma."

His heart hurt to the core even thinking about it. Talking about it…

"Come on, sweetheart. Talk to me."

"She thought I was trying to steal the bed and breakfast from her. She overheard me talking to Stone about paying it off so I could give it to her." He paused a moment to push down the emotion evident in his voice. "That she could think that about me after…she didn't trust me. A relationship can't be built on distrust."

His mom nodded. "Did you tell her what you'd done?"

"What did it matter? She believed I was capable of hurting her like that." He set his half-empty cup down. "That she would jump to that conclusion without even asking me about it…there was no fixing that."

"Did she even ask if you had an explanation?" His mom tilted her head. "It just seems out of character for her to not give you a chance."

She had, but his mom hadn't seen the look of total disgust in Reagan's eyes or heard it in her voice. The accusation had hit so hard, he'd been left winded. "She did, but, Mom, she wouldn't have believed me. Not after that."

"Honey, hadn't you been wanting to buy her home?"

"Well, yeah, at first. But not anymore. I wanted it fixed up and paid off. I wanted her to know I didn't want the bed and breakfast. I wanted her." And he'd ached for her every second since he'd left. She'd put a hole through his chest and hadn't seemed the least bit concerned.

"What *exactly* did you say to Stone?"

Shrugging, Hunter said, "I was telling Stone to gut two of the bedrooms. He asked me what I was doing, and I said I was fixing it up and then…" He squeezed his eyes shut and rubbed his face with his hands. "And then I said I was going to buy it. That I'd charmed it out of her." Now that he'd said it aloud, no wonder she'd been so angry, and now he understood her angry comment on her porch about charming it out of her.

His mom exhaled sharply. "Oh, Hunter, it sounds like based on what she heard and your history, she had good reason to think something was going on, especially when you didn't explain when she asked. Go back to Tybee and tell her. That girl loves you."

"Yeah, but one little misunderstanding and she walks out? How's that going to work for a marriage?"

His mom chuckled. "This is a hiccup. You think anything in marriage will be easy? I've got news for you, bucko: it's not. The arguments and disagreements will be worse because then you're living with the person you're upset with."

"I doubt she'd even give me that opportunity." In fact, he was sure of it.

"Then you need to decide if she's worth the risk. There's a chance she won't, but if you never try, you'll always wonder if she would have." His mom picked up her cup and stood. "You're going to have to put yourself out there, baby. Is she worth it or not? You're the only one who can make that call." Without another word, she left him on the porch.

He sat forward, his elbows on his knees and his head in his hands. What if he took his mom's advice? What if he put himself out there and she trampled on him like she had before? He could still feel the boots on his back as she'd walked over him.

He supposed he deserved it to a degree after the way he'd treated her about the money issue. She had put herself out there when she'd admitted to knowing, and he'd run her over just as badly. Would they ever be able to make it work after hurting each other like they had?

The one thing he couldn't deny was that he loved her and was miserable without her. Each day the misery seemed to pile higher, and it was getting harder to breathe the longer he was away from her.

Slowly, a plan formed. He'd take the chance. The other option, the life that didn't include her, wasn't a life he wanted.

He wanted her more than he wanted to keep his heart safe. He wanted her more than anything.

CHAPTER 24

Naomi dropped another dress on the bed. "You could wear this one."

Reagan shook her head. "No, it's dingy-looking."

"You should wear one of the dresses Carrie Anne gave you," Kaylee said as she continued to dig through Reagan's closet. The closet that had new doors and handles.

She had no idea the man-hours that went into it, but somehow Hunter had managed to take her beaten-up bed and breakfast and turn it into a showpiece. From the freshly painted ceiling to the newly sanded floors to the porch railing that promised not to dump someone over the side. Not only had he fixed up the home, but he'd had new appliances installed.

At first, she'd been so angry that all it did was make

her even more furious, but as the days passed, the anger subsided. In truth, he'd pulled a miracle, and it was wonderful. He'd even told them to make sure they kept the wall drawings. Now there were little frames here and there showing the drawings that were once hidden.

Along with the sweaters and shirts, Hunter's sister had given her a couple of dresses too. Boy, had she loved his family and loved being part of it. She picked up the soft green knee-length dress. When she'd tried it on in Caprock Canyon, it had fit so perfectly. Now it just made her heart hurt. "I don't know." She tossed it back on the bed.

"Reagan, you should talk to him. Maybe you heard him wrong, or maybe they were talking about it but it wasn't what you thought," Naomi said, taking her by the arms. "You claim to love him, but you didn't give him any opportunity to tell you what happened."

Reagan huffed. "Yes, I did. He said nothing." But she'd seen a world of hurt in his eyes. At the time, she'd been so angry she'd ignored it, but in the days following her accusations, the scene had played over and over in her mind. She pulled away from her friend.

Naomi crossed her arms. "Yeah, after accusing him.

Even if he had defended himself, would you have believed him? Be honest, Reagan."

Reagan cast her gaze to the bed, staring at the dress. No, she wouldn't have. The fury she'd felt held no room for mercy or understanding. If he'd said anything at that moment, she'd have found a way to throw it back in his face. "No," she whispered.

Kaylee hugged her. "I know you've been dealt a bad hand lately, but maybe…maybe just give him a real chance to explain. You love him. Both of us can see it."

Shrugging, Reagan sighed. "Maybe. For now, I need to get dressed for the mayor's whatever-it-is."

In an effort to get tourism back in swing, the mayor was having all the businesses affected by the hurricane meet on the beach. He was bringing in marketing experts, and since she had absolutely no funds for that, she'd decided to go. Even if she was on the fence as to whether she wanted to keep the bed and breakfast or not, if it was showing signs of being successful, maybe it would sell for a better price *if* she decided to sell.

Once she was dressed, she slipped on one of the sweaters that matched the dress Carrie Anne had given her. Part of her wore it because it fit; the other part because the smell of Caprock Canyon clung to it.

Hugging herself, she set out for the meeting,

contemplating what she needed to do about Hunter. She missed him. Missed his smile. His blue eyes. His calloused hands. All of him.

As she reached the area designated for the gathering, she slowed. There was a single table with seating for two and a lone candle flickering in the breeze. Movement from the side caught her attention, and Hunter walked into view. Blood rushed in her ears, and her lips parted as she gasped.

"Hunter?"

With his hands in his slack pockets, he approached and stopped a foot or so away. "I wanted it fixed up because I wanted you to be free to choose whether you stayed or not."

"Free to choose?" Her voice was barely audible above the crash of the waves.

He nodded, continuing. "What you overheard me talking about was surprising you with the house being fixed and then offering to pay off the mortgage. I wanted to pay off the loan for you. Not take it from you."

Stunned silence was all she had as she tried to process what he was saying. "For me?"

"Yeah. I tried to get the bank to let me pay off the note, but I had to have your permission. I wanted to give it to you before I told you I loved you because I wanted you to know that you are all I wanted."

Tears pooled in her eyes. "Hunter—"

Holding up his hand, he stopped her. "I'd been trying to buy it. From your perspective, I can see why you would have thought—"

"No." She stepped closer to him. "I should have trusted you. I should have come to you, told you what I heard, and listened. Instead, I immediately jumped to a conclusion I knew, deep in my heart, you weren't capable of. You are kind, gentle, and warm. I've been freezing to death since you left."

He took a deep breath. "You think we could communicate better in the future?"

"I know so." She rushed forward and threw her arms around him. "I love you, Hunter. I love you with all my heart."

Wrapping his arms around her, he buried his face in her neck. "I love you, Reagan."

The tiny yip of a puppy made her lean back. The little bark got closer and closer. She looked up at Hunter. "You didn't."

His smile was almost as bright as the sliver of moon in the sky. "I kinda had help with all of this."

A brown Great Dane puppy stopped at her feet, and its little tail wagged so hard it was a whip. She scooped him into her arms, and her smile faded as she saw the collar…and the ring.

When she looked at Hunter, he dropped to one knee. "I love you. You're the only one I want. Captain and I would be incredibly honored if you'd marry us."

A tiny half-laugh, half-cry popped out. "Captain?"

"It's a great name, and because I'm totally in love with you, we'll go with that."

Through a haze of tears, she nodded. "Captain's the name, and I'd love to marry you."

Hunter stood, unclipped Captain's collar, and took the ring off. He slipped it on her finger and refastened the collar. "You've made the two of us very happy."

Captain whined, and Reagan hugged him. The puppy licked her face fast and furiously. She giggled as Hunter slipped his arm around her waist and kissed her. A wiggly puppy didn't make for the longest engagement kiss, but it did make it the best.

"I love you, sweetheart. Home is wherever you are."

She cupped his cheek. "I love you too, and I feel the same way."

EPILOGUE

Eight months later...

Josiah laid his hand on Hunter's shoulder. "Relax, bud. It's going to be okay."

It had been a hard decision when it came time to pick a best man. He loved all his brothers equally, and he didn't want any of them to feel slighted. He also had Bandit, Israel, Stone, and Ryan to consider as well. Then there was his dad.

In the end, he'd picked his brother Josiah. It had been a foolproof method. A game of cornhole, and Josiah had won.

"I'm fine," Hunter whispered back.

"Tell that to your sweaty forehead." Hunter's brother chuckled.

"Shut up. It's hot."

Josiah grunted a laugh and clasped his hands in front of him. "If you say so."

It wasn't nerves that had Hunter anxious. The Wedding March would play any second, and the wind had picked up. Reagan had wanted a beach wedding, and Hunter had made it happen. Now, he just needed the weather to cooperate long enough for him to kiss the bride.

Naomi stopped at the opposite end of the runner and gave two thumbs up. *Perfect,* she mouthed.

The disc jockey took his cue and started the track. First came Carlin, Reagan's sister, and then followed Naomi, Kaylee, Gabby, and Carrie Anne, one by one escorted by the groomsmen. Of course, Captain was next with the rings safely hooked to his collar. His ears flopped as he trotted to the front and stopped at Hunter's feet.

It had taken some intense training to get him ring-bearer ready, but it was worth it. Hunter and Reagan had taken the class together, and they'd learned a lot about dogs and each other.

Finally, Reagan was at the end of the runner, arm hooked in her dad's. Hunter liked Reagan's parents. They were definitely different from his, but they were good people.

Her dad handed him Reagan's hand, and Hunter smiled at her. How he'd managed to snag the most beautiful woman in the world was still a mystery to him. There still wasn't a day when she wasn't more beautiful than the last.

This was it, and he'd never felt more peace in his life.

When she reached him, her dad paused before stepping back. "This is my little girl. Take care of her."

"I will."

The rest of the ceremony was a blur. They'd decided to stick with traditional vows. Not that they didn't have the ability to write something different, but they both liked traditions.

As soon as the minister said Hunter could kiss the bride, he pulled her close and kissed her. With the introduction of them as Mr. and Mrs. West, their families cheered as Captain barked and wagged his tail.

Hunter leaned in, set his lips to her ear, and whispered, "I love you."

She kissed him and palmed the side of his face. "I love you too."

Life with her was going to be an adventure. One he'd been aching for. Not only did he have the home by the ocean he'd dreamed of, but he had the woman he wanted too. Now that he had it, he was going to cherish it for as long as he lived.

For a list of all books by Bree Livingston, please visit her website at www.breelivingston.com.

ABOUT THE AUTHOR

Bree Livingston lives in the West Texas Panhandle with her husband, children, and cats. She'd have a dog, but they took a vote and the cats won. Not in numbers, but attitude. They wouldn't even debate. They just leveled their little beady eyes at her and that was all it took for her to nix getting a dog. Her hobbies include...nothing because she writes all the time.

She loves carbs, but the love ends there. No, that's not true. The love usually winds up on her hips which is why she loves writing romance. The love in the pages of her books are sweet and clean, and they definitely don't add pounds when you step on the scale. Unless of course, you're actually holding a Kindle while you're weighing. Put the Kindle down and try again. Also, the cookie because that could be the problem too. She knows from experience.

Join her mailing list to be the first to find out

publishing news, contests, and more by going to her website at https://www.breelivingston.com.

facebook.com/BreeLivingstonWrites

twitter.com/BreeLivWrites

bookbub.com/authors/bree-livingston